GERRY ANDERSON'S

WHITE STORM

GERRY ANDERSON'S

WHITE STORM
M. G. HARRIS

Orion
Children's Books

Orion Children's Books
First published in Great Britain in 2016 by Hodder and Stoughton

1 3 5 7 9 10 8 6 4 2

Copyright © Anderson Entertainment Media Limited, 2016

The moral rights of the author have been asserted.

A CIP catalogue record for this book
is available from the British Library

ISBN 978 1 4440 1410 5

Typeset by Input Data Services Ltd, Bridgwater, Somerset

Printed and bound by CPI Group (UK) Ltd, Croydon, CRO 4YY

The paper and board used in this book are from well-managed
forests and other responsible sources.

Orion Children's Books
An imprint of
Hachette Children's Group
Part of Hodder and Stoughton
Carmelite House
50 Victoria Embankment
London EC4Y 0DZ

An Hachette UK Company
www.hachette.co.uk

www.orionchildrensbooks.co.uk

For my brother Michael, who came up with Davos.
– M. G. Harris

For Dad – for entertaining and inspiring me and so many others, and for Mum – for encouraging and supporting us both every step of the way.
– Jamie Anderson

How Gerry Anderson's
Gemini Force One Got off the Ground

An introduction from
Gerry's younger son Jamie

After completing work on what would be his final television series (*New Captain Scarlet*) my father – Gerry Anderson (creator of cult classics like *Fireball XL5, Thunderbirds* and *Space: 1999*) – began work on a new sci-fi adventure series. However, this time it wasn't a TV series or a film . . . it was a novel.

As he worked I could see something really thrilling emerging. Something with all the excitement and adventure you might expect from an episode of his most famous creation – *Thunderbirds* – combined with a more modern feel that he'd started to explore in his *New Captain Scarlet* series.

Sadly, it soon became apparent to us – and to him – that he was already living with Alzheimer's disease. And so, over time, his progress on the book slowed.

Eventually he was forced to stop work as his ability to read and write was taken from him. It seemed so cruel that a man who loved nothing more than to write and create was no longer able to do so. Even so – his desire to get this final project rolling stuck with him right up until the end.

Dad died on 26th December 2012.

In the days and weeks after Dad's funeral, I began to piece together the projects he'd been working on before he was forced to abandon them due to his dementia. I really felt there was something special in this final project, and started to explore the possibility of getting it completed.

Not too long after I'd started working on it, I met with M.G. Harris. She wrote a treatment of the first few chapters using material Dad had left behind. When I read it, things suddenly felt like they'd fallen into place. The content, the dialogue, the pace . . . it all felt so authentic. We had our author! We also finally decided on a name for the project – Gemini Force One.

We approached a number of publishers, but we couldn't seem to find one who would take the project without changing so many elements of the story that it no longer felt like a Gerry Anderson creation. So we turned to the crowdfunding website, Kickstarter.

After a month of planning, we launched the campaign. The response blew us away. Over 600 fans from all over the world put their own hard-earned cash into our project to make sure we could complete and publish the book in the way that Dad would have wanted.

And the good news didn't stop there – a short time later, we had a very exciting meeting with Orion. They loved the book and, best of all, they didn't want to change it! Very soon, we'd struck a deal to publish Gemini Force One!

I'm amazed that so much has happened in such a short time, and that we're now in a position to introduce Gemini Force One to new and existing Gerry Anderson fans all over the world. I'm incredibly grateful to those who have helped us make this happen – all of our wonderful Kickstarter backers, M.G. Harris, our agent Robert Kirby, and of course Amber and the team at Orion.

Stand by for action!

~ A SMART MOVE ~

From the moment he swung for it, Ben could feel that he was being watched. His fist rocketed into the hanging punchbag, sent it swinging with a metallic whine as the chain that held it creaked. In the corner of his eye, he saw another teenage boy put down a dumb-bell. Even with his attention on the punchbag, Ben sensed the boy's gaze.

He pivoted slightly so that the other boy completely dropped out of his field of vision, and continued to throw punches. Some liked to be watched during a workout, but not Ben. He preferred just to get on with it, not to be drawn into some time-wasting discussion about how much weight and how many reps and what brand of protein shake.

In quick succession he threw three vicious punches. Each hit an imaginary target: Minos Winter, the mercenary who'd blown up the Horizon Alpha drilling platform. Richard Mokwene, the leader of a gang of illegal gold miners. That piece-of-junk drug trafficker whose greed had caused Ben's mother to drown. Each one of these men had brought Ben pain. Theirs were the faces he imagined when he struck out. Each blow connected with utter precision, each one heavier than the last.

'Would be more fun if you were hitting me, no?' said a voice, suddenly at his side. Ben startled at the sound, his final strike glancing off the edge of the bag. He turned to see that the boy who'd been observing him was now right next to him.

The boy was almost as tall as Ben and looked to be somewhere between sixteen and eighteen. He was slightly overweight, thickset, with spiky blond hair and a ski-tan that reached in a V-shape to just below his throat. Strangely enough, the boy addressed Ben in English, even though they were in Austria.

'I speak German,' Ben told him.

'That's cool,' the boy replied, switching to German. 'In German then; would you prefer to be hitting a person? Because you and me, we can do that.'

Ben flushed, beginning to sweat as his body relaxed from the workout. 'Hit you? Uh, no thanks, pal.' He tried to smile, which was difficult, because the other boy's stony-faced stare didn't waver.

'It takes more skill to hit a person,' the blond boy reasoned. His blue-grey eyes narrowed, but otherwise the boy's flat, even features remained impassive. 'A *person* can dodge.'

'I'm good with the bag, thanks all the same,' Ben said. What he wanted to say was 'what's your problem?'. He tried to turn his attention away from the teenager, but there he was, crowding the space to Ben's right.

'I'm making you angry, right?' The faintest hint of a

smirk touched the other boy's lips. 'Why not see where that anger takes us both?'

'Easy, tiger,' said a third voice, languid and amused. Ben flicked his head to the left, relieved to see his Gemini Force crew-mate, Addison Nicole Dyer. The twenty-something pilot sauntered over from where she'd been exercising with kettle bells, her lithe, slight form dressed in grey-and-red lycra. Her shoulder-length, bobbed dark brown hair was damp with sweat from the workout and strands of it were plastered to her neck, but otherwise Addi looked supremely relaxed. She grinned, lazily, at the second boy. 'You seen how hard this dude hits? Trust me; you don't want him throwing a punch at that pretty face.'

If the second boy enjoyed the surely ironic compliment, it didn't show. 'I can hit hard too,' he said, matching Addison's English.

'Hey look, I don't want to hurt you,' Ben said.

'You won't,' the boy replied, deadpan.

'Really,' Ben countered, smiling the charming smile he'd learned from his father. 'I appreciate the offer. But I'm just here to work out. I don't fight.'

The boy hesitated. When it seemed clear that Ben wasn't joking, he turned and stalked off.

Addison gave a conspiratorial chuckle. 'Seriously?'

Ben swivelled back to the punchbag and threw his fist; a right hook. The bag flew across the exercise space. They both stepped aside as it swung back.

'I think Frying-Pan Face liked you.'

'Yeah, right,' muttered Ben. He wondered if Addison knew how often he'd been accosted in public gyms, competitive guys who wanted to show off how much stronger or faster they were. After months of hard training with the crew of Gemini Force, his body had adapted to the physical rigour. He didn't look like your average body-conscious sixteen-year-old, sleek and ripped like a pop star; Ben was merely lean and hard, with biceps and shoulders formed more from combat training than from weights. He seemed to bring out a competitive urge in some boys.

The bag arced away from them. Ben shrugged. 'Everyone's got something to prove.'

'Truby's outside,' Addison said. 'Wants to take us all out to dinner to celebrate your deal. It's not every day that a rich kid gives away his fortune to educate the poor.'

'I haven't signed the contract yet,' Ben pointed out. 'Maybe I'll change my mind.'

Addison glanced at him in surprise. 'You'd do that? What about Zama-Zula and all those South African miners' kids? Haven't you gotten them all excited by the plans for the new school you're going to build there?'

'It's a joke,' Ben said, reddening. With his teeth, he pulled apart the Velcro strips that held his boxing glove in place. Course I'm going to sign.' The contracts he'd be signing would put two million Euros to work in a charity he'd started. Ben would never let Zula down, or the other children of the *zama-zama*, the illegal gold miners that he'd helped escape from the hellish depths of one of the world's deepest mines.

'It's a dope move, kid,' Addison said. 'Not gonna lie – you definitely get my vote for philanthropist of the year.'

Ben didn't reply. He removed the second glove and made his way across the gym to the men's changing room. He didn't particularly enjoy discussing money with anyone in Gemini Force. The fact that he'd been born into Austrian aristocracy, as well as being the son of a British multi-millionaire, was always going to set Benedict Carrington apart from his crew-mates in Gemini Force. Even Jason Truby, the billionaire who'd founded the secret rescue agency, hadn't been born to his fortune.

Throughout the life of his late mother, Countess Caroline Brandis-Carrington, their ancestral home in Austria, Schloss Bach, had exerted a powerful draw. Now that he'd inherited the title of 'Count Brandis', Ben felt something similar. He didn't like it.

Gemini Force was his life now, and its base, GF One, was the centre of his universe. He wanted to let go of everything else. He didn't want to think about the cost of repairs, of gardeners, of interior decoration. Most of all though, he couldn't stop thinking about how all that money could and *should* be used to help people who really needed it.

Like the families of the illegal miners that Gemini Force had rescued in South Africa.

Why should Ben have all that cash, just because of an accident of birth? It wasn't as though he needed it, now that he was living on Gemini Force One.

Two million euros could change the lives of dozens of kids in Zama-Zula's village. It could prevent them having to become illegal miners, like their parents.

So Ben had decided to set up a charity and put Zula in charge. And yet, it didn't feel all that heroic to let go of the niggling feeling that he should be taking care of his mother's family home. Addison talked as though he was doing something noble. It made him feel faintly embarrassed. She'd fought in a war, flown fighter jets, risked her life to protect her country against terrorism.

Everyone in Gemini Force had a more impressive background than Ben.

After he'd showered and changed, Ben headed for the coffee bar of the luxury hotel in which they were staying, in the ski resort of St Anton am Arlberg. Fellow members of Gemini Force, Jason Truby, Michael Dietz, Toru Takitani and Addison were seated in a booth. In front of each of them was a steaming glass of Austrian mulled wine - *gluwein*.

Ben took a breath and headed over to join them.

There would always be people who looked at Ben just the way that Austrian boy had, wanting to prove to him that he wasn't *all that*. After his part in a number of high risk rescues, he knew he'd earned the respect of his crew-mates. He could feel it in the way they spoke to him, the way they increasingly trusted him to take on more responsibility.

But he wanted more. Ben wanted to earn everything he was. *Everything*.

THE WHOLE
NINE YARDS

'Hey kid, don't tell me you gave away two million bucks just to impress a girl.'

Addison turned to Ben with a quirky grin. They stood in the car park of Collège du Léman, an international school situated near the southern shores of Lake Geneva. Fifteen-year-old Jasmine Dietz was a student there. As the daughter of Michael Dietz, Gemini Force's chief of operations, she was the only girl Ben had spent any decent amount of time with since he'd joined Truby's secret global rescue agency.

'Not two million dollars,' Ben said. 'It was Euros.'

'Ha ha,' replied Addison. 'Huge difference, *not*.'

Behind them was the Mercedes GL-class seven-seater that Jason Truby had rented for the duration of their stay in Europe. Inside, Truby was talking on the phone.

Nervously, Ben licked his lips. He hadn't seen Jasmine since the new year – weeks ago. He'd liked her for ages, but had only realised just how much when he'd emerged from the hellish, sweltering cavern that was the Nomzamo gold mine in South Africa. Rescuing the illegal gold miners had made him understand how shallow so much of what passed as 'love tokens' could be. Gold was a metal that represented blood and sweat and greed, not love.

In Ben's mind, the journey from thoughts of *love* to thoughts of Jasmine was a short one.

But he had zero idea of how to tell her. Or if he even should. So – nervousness. That was going to be Ben's new reality, in Jasmine's presence.

It kind of sucked.

'Two million,' Addison repeated, slowly. 'That'll buy a *bunch* of admiration.'

Ben tried to object. 'That's not why I did it.'

'Doesn't even matter. Like I said, it's a smart move, either way. You get to help those kids in South Africa, you get to show Jasmine how generous you can be.'

Before Ben could respond, there was Jasmine, right in front of him, a huge smile on her face, her arms open to welcome him into a hug. He clasped her to him for a moment, registering a quickening of his heartbeat that had never been present in any of their previous embraces. He'd have stayed like that even longer, but the curious eyes of Jasmine's father, Dietz, were already settling on him.

Pulling back, Ben arranged his features into something he hoped looked pleasant and relaxed. A slow, casual 'Hey' was all he could manage, stopping himself quickly when he felt a catch in his voice. 'How's it going?'

'Really well,' Jasmine admitted, with a smile like sunshine. 'How's Rigel?'

Ben smiled back, delighted that her first question

was about his beloved flat-coated retriever. 'He's good. Brought him over for a bit of mountain air, you remember how much he likes his mountains, does Rigel.'

'And how about you, Mister Carnegie?'

Confused, Ben said, 'Who?'

'The big philanthropist? The American guy who gave away all his money? Well, like ninety percent of it, anyhow.'

'Oh - Ben's got ol' Andrew Carnegie beat.' Addison quipped. 'He gave away the whole nine yards.'

Ben grinned his most casual, modest smile. 'One does what one can.'

Jasmine rolled her eyes and sighed, clutching one hand to her heart in a melodramatic gesture. 'I do like it when you go all *Britischer*.'

He blinked, dazzled. It was like seeing her for the first time. As though admitting to himself that Jasmine actually meant something to him had somehow altered her physical appearance. Her hair seemed more lustrous, long chestnut tresses draped adorably over her shoulders. Her eyes were brighter, the faint glow of whiteness from the surrounding snow setting them off like jewels.

He opened the passenger door for her, wondering at the trembling of his heart. Addison had to physically push him into the car, following Jasmine.

'OK, next stop, CERN,' Truby said, from behind the wheel of the car. 'We should be there in a just over fifteen minutes. Dietz and I have a meeting scheduled.

You guys can hang out in the campus coffee shop. Then it's back to Geneva, hotel, and tomorrow, back to GF One.'

'You're going to CERN? Why?' Jasmine asked.

Ben's attention zeroed in on what Truby was saying. He'd overheard Truby and Dietz talking about the latest addition to Gemini Force's superb rescue equipment, but their chats usually got pretty technical and jargon-filled.

'We've been working with some nuclear scientists,' Truby replied. 'Professor Gerald Anderson has one of his research groups there. They've made a breakthrough in adapting smaller generators to use ganymedian. We should be able to fit the component they've developed into GF Nine - our new ice-digging vehicle.'

'OK,' Jasmine said. 'So anyway, what else is new?'

Ben was relieved to have something important-sounding to tell. They'd been in Europe for several days now, he told her, they'd flown across the Atlantic in GF Two – known as *Leo*.

'Lucky for you,' Jasmine said. 'I've always wanted to fly in *Leo*.'

It was the biggest aircraft in the Gemini Force stable, capable of carrying even their helicopter vehicle, GF Three, known as *Scorpio*, in its wide open central chamber. On this particular crossing, however, they'd flown with GF Nine – a vehicle adapted to melting and cutting through ice, and to slicing through hard-packed snow, reducing it to pellets that were jettisoned from the machine. The vehicle seemed to showcase a few other life-saving technologies too, of which Ben had only caught the occasional excited mutterings between Dietz and the medics during training sessions.

He was about to tell Jasmine all about GF Nine, when Truby's phone sounded over the car's stereo system. The next voice they heard was that of James Winch.

'This is *Cancer* on GF One,' he said. 'How close is *Leo* to the Jungfraujoch weather station? There's been a plane crash. Looks like something's gone into the tunnel inside the Eiger. It's bad. Train crash, plane crash, all of it high up on a mountain face. You might be able to help.'

～ON DUTY～

'At an elevation of 3,454 metres, the Jungfraujoch railway station is the highest in Europe,' Ben read aloud from his smartphone. 'Jazz, have you ever been?'

'A few times. I've skied in resorts near there; Wengen and Kleine Scheidegg. Kleine Scheidegg for fun; Wengen to train on the run they use for the Lauberhorn downhill race. Do you know it?'

'That's some serious downhill skiing,' Ben said, impressed. He wasn't a huge ski fan, but even he'd heard of the Lauberhorn ski races. That run wasn't for the faint-hearted. He knew that Jasmine was a major talent in the sport of ski cross, but if she could make any kind of time on the Lauberhorn run, she had to be pretty hardcore.

'Jasmine, since you know the region,' Truby instructed, 'I want you to grab my phone. James is going to send a link to someone who's streaming it as live video. Tell me what you see. There are no news crews out there yet. The live stream is from someone on the mountain, probably a skier who's gone off-piste.'

Jasmine touched her fingertip to the link that had just appeared on the screen of Truby's phone. It was part of a text message from James Winch, a geological engineer stationed at Gemini Force One. The screen filled with a shaky, slightly blurred image of smoke coiling in a background of white. Ben peered closely, trying to make out the images. It looked like chaos.

Jasmine began by turning the phone upside down, horizontally. 'Whoever's filming this, they've got the camera upside down. OK. This looks like the mouth of the tunnel that goes into the Eiger mountain. There's a funicular railway that goes from Kleine Scheidegg, up into the wall of the Eiger and then across to the Jungfraujoch weather station, which is on the ridge between the Mönch and the Jungfrau mountains. I'm guessing that the accident must be inside the tunnel because – look at all that smoke that's coming from inside it.'

Ben said, 'But I thought this was about a plane crash?'

Jasmine shook her head, doubtful. 'If the woman who's filming this would zoom out a little bit, maybe we could see more. Even if she'd move the camera some. But she's being really, really still. It's strange.'

Ben said, 'She?'

'The channel this is being streamed from apparently belongs to a woman,' Addison said. 'And Jazz is right. I'm getting a bad feeling about this. Look how close those snowflakes are, in the foreground, all out-of-focus? It's like she zoomed in as much as she could, started recording and uploading. And then . . .'

'Maybe she dropped the camera, but had to get out of there fast?' Jasmine suggested.

Addison nodded. 'Hopefully.'

The phone rang again. 'We're getting more details,' came James's voice. 'Looks like the plane actually flew into the side of the tunnel. A few heli-skiers who were higher up on the slopes have reached Kleine Scheidegg. They're reporting seeing a small jet-powered aircraft flying over from the direction of the Schilthorn mountain. It changed course last minute on the approach to the north face of the Eiger, seemed to accelerate and then flew straight into the side of the mountain.'

'Holy heck,' murmured Addison. 'That's messed up.'

'It's worse,' admitted James, and Ben could hear the reluctance to continue in his voice. 'Other skiers reported seeing a train going into the tunnel a few seconds before.'

Addison sucked her breath in sharply, while Jasmine said, 'Oh no – the plane crashed into the train, too?'

'I think we have to assume the worst here,' Truby said, his voice tight. 'The next question is – what can we do to help?'

For the first time, Michael Dietz spoke up. He'd been watching over his daughter's shoulder, silent as he assessed the situation. 'The emphasis has to be on getting people out of there ASAP. The local mountain rescue crews will already be on their way. But what they need is fire-fighting equipment and metal-cutting equipment. With *Leo* already in Europe and carrying GF Nine,' Dietz hesitated. 'I mean, if we were cutting through snow and ice, maybe. But this happened inside a tunnel. It's more a matter of getting crew and medics onto the site. Without at least a chopper, there's not much we can do to help.'

Truby made a clicking noise of irritation. 'A heli won't be difficult. We can pick up some rescue equipment from *Leo*.'

'Your next problem is going to be landing the chopper. The railway line there isn't flat – hence the funicular system.'

'We'll take skis and drop out. Everyone can ski OK, right?'

'Including me,' Jasmine said, a little timidly. 'Maybe . . . maybe I can help on this one?'

'I was thinking that we could use someone good to ski injured people down to the resort,' Truby said. With every word the founder of Gemini Force spoke, Ben could sense the growing resolve, the determination that his team would find a way to help at the scene of what surely had to be a gruesome disaster. 'We'll use those rescue sleds. *Leo* carries a couple. You need to be strong as well as an excellent skier. Jasmine, you think you can handle that?'

Jasmine nodded, firmly. 'I think so.'

The Mercedes GL seven-seater turned off the motorway. Then Truby was heading back the way they'd come, on the E-25.

'We'll rent a heli at the Payerne airbase where we parked *Leo*, pick up what we need and head on over to the Jungfraujoch. ETA won't be better'n ninety minutes or so, but I'm guessing those guys can use all the help they can get.'

'Rigel comes too, right?' Ben asked, hoping. He was pretty sure that the dog was still asleep in the rear of the vehicle, where he'd last seen him. But that was fine – Rigel could be roused to full alertness within seconds, an ability for which Ben rather envied his canine fellow rescue worker.

Ben could feel a steady pulse of adrenaline beginning to work through his veins, making the muscles of his thighs twitch in anticipation of the exertion ahead. In his mind he was already carrying a survivor through steep snow. He tried not to think about the injuries that people would have inside there. Mostly, he succeeded at blocking such thoughts. Imagination served a purpose, he'd found, but only up to a point. In each situation he'd found that the best attitude was one of alert acceptance. You had to be ready for anything, but not worry too much in advance.

It was one of the worst things about working as a rescuer, but also the best. You could never completely relax. The challenge, excitement and danger of the job were always on the horizon. However, since Gemini Force's underwater base, GF One, was situated sixty-four kilometres off the coast of the Mexican island of Cozumel, Ben occasionally allowed himself to be lulled into a 'holiday feeling'. That feeling, he now realised, was entirely wrong.

So long as they could marshal enough force and equipment to a rescue scene, Gemini Force was on duty everywhere, all the time.

➤ SECOND THOUGHTS ➤

They reached Payerne, the Swiss military airbase at which Truby had negotiated landing rights for GF Two. Unless they were actively engaged in a rescue, they'd park Gemini Force One craft in a NATO base. Truby's mysterious red-haired friend in the US government, 'Emma', appeared to have smoothed the way. In NATO bases, no questions were asked.

But Switzerland wasn't part of NATO. The military answered only to the Swiss. Ben had no idea how Truby had managed to persuade the Swiss to allow GF Two into one of their military airbases. At least, not without asking awkward questions about where a telecoms billionaire like Jason Truby would lay his hands on technology that even the US Department of Defence would officially deny existed.

Then again, Truby could be incredibly persuasive.

Ben's mother, Countess Caroline Brandis-Carrington, had wanted her own rescue agency. Truby had convinced her to join forces. He'd made a compelling case. There'd also been the small matter of the Carrington family's bankruptcy, Ben reflected. Bankruptcy, plus the fact that by then, Caroline was probably in love with Truby.

These thoughts rattled through Ben's head as he pulled

on his Gemini Force uniform, zipping up the anthracite grey jacket over a black Rock Snakes of Mars T-shirt. Thinking about his mother often made him sad. Ben sometimes tried to resist. It was never easy, especially in the Alps, where they'd both grown up.

Ben pulled himself out of his memories and turned his attention to Jasmine. She'd changed into a figure-hugging, one-piece blue-and-red ski suit, and was choosing a pair of skis from one of *Leo*'s equipment lockers. She seemed to be lost in concentration.

'Powder, big mountain or free-ride?' she asked, with a glance at Ben.

'Mum bought big mountain and powder skis for the Caroliners,' he mused. 'I trained with both.' He hesitated. 'It's pretty steep up there. I think big mountain would be the thing for most of the descent. But, you're going to be coming down on the piste, as well as in the deep snow. So maybe you should go for free-ride, and the rest of us take big mountain.'

'Makes sense.' She gave him a shy nod and then her fingers darted nimbly between the various skis, picking out three pairs. 'Jason told me to get skis for me, you and Toru. Addison's going to pilot the helicopter. Truby's going in there with the fire suit.'

Ben make a choking noise as he gasped. 'Truby's getting involved? He's getting into the fire suit? Does he think he's Tony frikkin' Stark?'

When Jasmine didn't reply, but instead gazed at him with limpid, wide eyes, Ben froze. Slowly he turned to find Truby standing less than two metres away, a bemused grin on his lips.

'Who's Tony Stark?' asked Truby, convincingly enough that Ben wasn't sure whether he was serious. If anyone else in Gemini Force had said that, Ben might have snarked them, or at least waited for Addison to have a go. But no one snarked Jason Truby to his face. It wasn't out of fear, but a genuine and deep-seated respect, as well as a healthy dose of wariness.

Ben felt the hideous crawl of embarrassment sweeping across his neck and face. 'Well, y'know, we sometimes call the fire suit the "Iron Man suit", hence the reference.'

Truby made a tutting sound and lowered his eyes, shaking his head sadly a couple of times. 'You really think I don't know who Tony Stark is? Ben – who wouldn't want to play at being Iron Man? But this suit, I'm afraid to say, works in the real world, not the comic book world. And in the real world, our technology is a heck of a lot more limited.'

'Still pretty amazing though,' Ben said, thinking back to how he'd watched Paul Scott flying around the blazing inferno of a burning oil refinery in the jet-packed fire suit, zapping critical points with blasts of liquid nitrogen from nozzles in the arms of the suit. 'I didn't know you'd trained in the suit,' he admitted.

'Give me credit,' said Truby, in a voice that was uncharacteristically playful. 'I wasn't going to let our boys Paul and Toru have all the fun, now was I?'

'It's *not* fun,' Michael Dietz said, shortly. He'd wandered over from the pilot controls on the other side of GF Two, and was leaning with his left shoulder against a closed locker door. 'Jason, you should reconsider. Or let Toru do it – he's a flyboy, at least.'

'We need Toru on skis,' Truby said, all humour draining from his voice. 'And we also need someone to get as far into that tunnel as the heat will allow. I'm doing it and that's all.'

Ben raised an eyebrow. 'Didn't know Toru skied,' he murmured to Jasmine after Truby and Dietz had left to get Truby into the multi-piece fire suit.

'He's better than me,' she replied. 'Toru was raised in a remote Japanese village. It would get cut off at winter, except for ski access. Real snow country.'

They were ready in another ten minutes. Ben checked his Gemini Force-issue Breitling Avenger watch; it had been seventy minutes since Truby had turned the car around on the E-25. In that time he'd achieved the impressive feat of driving like a crazed loon on the motorway all the way to the airbase, without being picked up for speeding by the Swiss traffic police. Then he'd talked someone at the base into loaning them a Eurocopter EC635 helicopter. By the time Ben had joined the rest of the team inside GF Two, they'd assembled their kit and were dressed, including pale grey, ultra-light Salomon ski boots which they wore unbuckled at the top.

Dietz, Toru, Ben, Jasmine and Truby climbed into the Eurocopter. Its blades were already rotating, slowly, as Addison warmed the craft up.

Ben and Jasmine sat side-by-side, jammed between the outer door, two boxes of medical equipment and all the skis. The helicopter began to lift off the ground. He had to use one arm to prevent the skis from falling against Jasmine's back as the craft tilted when Addison adjusted the pitch controls. In Gemini Force's own customised helicopter, *Scorpio*, there were wall-mounted racks for all kinds of equipment. But this was the medical evacuation version of the Eurocopter EC635. Most of the storage space had been adapted to take two medical litters and advanced first aid equipment, as well as five seated medical workers.

Everyone in Gemini Force knew first aid, but Ben had only just begun the training. And Jasmine wasn't even part of the rescue agency, only related to its chief of operations. As he held the weight of the skis barely five millimetres from her shoulder, Ben managed to grin at Jasmine, wishing he'd thought of putting his own back against the uncomfortable equipment.

'What's wrong?' she asked, suddenly frowning. 'Are the skis too heavy?'

'No,' Ben lied, holding back a grunt from the effort of taking the weight of six large skis, bindings and poles in one hand.

If she doubted his word, Jasmine didn't show it. Instead she flashed him the most adorably grateful smile.

Ben exhaled suddenly, unaware that he'd been holding his breath.

For the first time, he allowed thoughts of what they were about to find to crowd into his mind; thoughts that he'd kept at bay quite successfully until just now. It was the best way; to concentrate on the details of preparation, not to imagine in any detail what lay ahead. Now though, so close to the reality, it was impossible to resist his imagination.

Memories assailed him, from the time Gemini Force had performed a rescue at a burning oil refinery. *Fire.* A flash of recollection: the taste of acrid, choking smoke seemed to fill his mouth. The prickle of his skin as the air around him began to burn.

Fire. Snow. Blood. This was going to be grim. A quick glance into the eyes of Truby and Dietz, who sat opposite, confirmed Ben's suspicions. They knew it, too.

The feeling that Ben had then took him totally by surprise. He was actually having second thoughts. He looked at Jasmine, really looked. There was no apprehension in her eyes. Instead they were bright and alive. Eager, excited. And he felt a surge of anger. His eyes went straight to Dietz's. This time Ben glared at him in silent accusation.

Dietz knew what they were likely to find up on that mountain. How could he send his own daughter into that? What kind of friend was Ben, to even think of leading someone young, untrained and unseasoned - straight into hell?

CRASH SITE

'I think maybe when we get to the crash site, Jasmine should stay in the chopper,' Ben said, trying to make it sound like the most reasonable suggestion possible. 'Don't you reckon, Dietz? Addison's piloting, Truby's wearing the fire suit, Toru will ski down with any survivors. You're the only one who'd be here to treat any injuries. I'm pretty sure you could use an extra hand?'

He'd been a bit apprehensive about how Jasmine might take this. But nothing had prepared him for the look of sheer vitriol and disbelief that she shot him. It took her a few seconds to recover from the obvious shock, seconds during which, Ben noticed, Dietz merely gazed at Ben with a highly amused expression. It was practically triumphant.

'What?' she managed to blurt, after a moment. 'Did you just tell me that I can't get involved in a rescue? Benedict Carrington - seriously?'

In the seats opposite, Dietz said nothing, but it was obviously costing him some effort to keep the smirk on his face from erupting into outright laughter.

From the pilot seat, Ben could hear the quiet rumble of laughter from Addison and then she muttered, 'Dude . . . not cool. Not cool at all.'

'Helping the injured people is being part of the rescue,' Ben objected, but it sounded pretty half-hearted. 'I'm serious. There are lots of ways to be a rescuer. You don't have to be the one to physically drag survivors from some hellhole.'

'That's absolutely true and I'm *delighted* to hear you say it,' Dietz said, drily. 'And yet, Ben, you've always preferred to do just that.'

Ben was already regretting what he'd said. But he couldn't help how he felt. Just the thought of what Jasmine might see. The idea of her being caught in flames or smoke, of some accident befalling her on the treacherous route down to the resort of Kleine Scheidegg. It had tripped something in Ben, and he'd spoken without thinking. Now he had to make it sound like a sensible suggestion, and not a load of sexist rubbish.

'Once we get people out of that tunnel,' Truby said, finally speaking up, '*if* we get anyone out, Ben, which is a possible outcome that you need to begin to accept, then trust me, once we've taken one survivor on board in the litter, Jasmine and Toru are the best bet for getting anyone else down the mountain.'

Ben sunk back in his seat, stony-faced, flushed with embarrassment. He couldn't bear even to glance at Jasmine, although he did notice that she had deliberately turned, apparently peering out of the window with intense purpose. He shifted a little, swallowed hard, trying to find something to say, something that didn't make things even worse. It was useless. There was nothing but awkwardness there.

By the time he felt the hot rush of indignation and shame recede, Ben noticed the approach, on the horizon, of the familiar wall of the Bernese Oberland range of the Alps. He and Jasmine had skied there only a few weeks ago, part of a training mission for Ben and Rigel. Although he hadn't known it at the time – the test had been more for Rigel's benefit than Ben's. Memories of swimming in a freezing cold underground river sent a shudder through him, strong enough for Jasmine to notice.

'What's wrong, are the skis getting too heavy?'

For the first time since his outburst, Ben allowed himself to look at Jasmine. He'd been expecting to find something akin to a sneer in her expression, but it wasn't like that at all. She seemed genuinely concerned.

'I was just remembering that horrible, freezing cold river,' he admitted. Jasmine, Ben remembered, had actually been ultra-calm, determined. He'd worried about her then, too. But that time it had been guilt about being the one who'd made a bad decision, one that might have put them in serious danger.

Feelings! They made it so difficult to stay focused. He stared out of the window, pretending to find something utterly fascinating in the approach of the Alpine peaks.

'Oh hello, here's the Jungfrau,' he murmured.

'That river was the worst,' Jasmine said, after a while. 'But Rigel was amazing. Both of you, working as a team. You got us out of there.'

Ben tried to say something then, something about how he wanted to keep her safe, but the words wouldn't even assemble in his brain.

'Benedict,' Truby said, his voice low, almost a warning. 'Time to concentrate. Let's all go over the plan one more time.'

As the chopper swooped down towards the ridge of craggy peaks in the Bernese Oberland, the crash site came into view. You couldn't miss it – a thick pall of black smoke twisted upwards, flattening somewhere beneath a bank of clouds that floated above the summits of the Jungfrau and Mönch. Most of the smoke was gushing out of the tunnel, but almost as much was roiling around the blazing wreckage of an aeroplane. The nose of the burning, broken aircraft was buried in a jagged hole in the pure white slope of the mountain. Lower down the slope were the first rescue crew, dotted around the snow. Four snowmobiles carried two people each. Two more were fitted with rigs for hauling some kind of equipment - for fire-fighting, Ben guessed. Since it was nowhere to be seen, he assumed it was already in use inside the tunnel.

On board with Gemini Force, no one spoke. The horrors of a disaster site couldn't be articulated with anything that approached accuracy. Dark jokes might come to mind, but no one in Gemini Force, as far as he knew, ever resorted to morbid humour. And he was glad of it.

Addison flew them in low towards the crease

between the north wall of the Eiger and the slopes of the neighbouring mountains. The smoke thickened. Without a word, everyone reached for the breathing masks they'd brought on board, fastening them into place. When Ben finished adjusting his mask, he saw that Jasmine was looking at him through the toughened, clear plastic. Instinctively, he reached for her hand, intertwined their fingers and squeezed.

'Be careful,' he managed to say, adding, in an urgent whisper, 'Please.'

The Eurocopter EC635 came to a hovering standstill, about twenty metres above the steep incline of snow and less than thirty metres from the yawning black hole from which smoke gushed; the mouth of the tunnel in the Eiger.

Truby rose first, waited as Dietz attached the jet pack to the back of the fire suit. Then he moved to the door and threw the handle, sliding the door. He stepped outside, lowered himself onto the landing skids. The instant that the jet pack was clear of the structure of the chopper, they heard a flaming roar as Truby ignited the pack. Then he was off – flying low over the snow as he zoomed towards the mouth of the tunnel.

Piloting the craft, Addison followed close behind Truby, until they were only ten metres away. A breeze was wafting the thick smoke away, back towards the mountain, or else they wouldn't have been able to fly any closer.

Ben stood, placed his skis onto the floor of the

helicopter and snapped one boot and then the other into the bindings. Beside him, Rigel looked up with trusting eyes. They were hovering almost two metres above the snow now; low enough that it was possible to jump out of the chopper and ski. He flexed his leg muscles and grabbed two poles. Toru was already at the edge, preparing to launch himself outside. A second later he'd gone.

'Rigel – leap of faith!' Ben yelled, with an encouraging shove to the dog's hind quarters. It was hardly necessary, as Rigel was already yapping with excitement as he threw himself after Toru, onto the snow.

Ben was next. He flashed Jasmine a quick grin, took a breath and then jumped.

Landing, he felt the impact judder through his entire frame. His skis sank in the deep snow, to the depth of his boots. He grabbed hold of Rigel and attached the dog's breathing mask. Rigel whined only slightly; a highly controlled response because Ben knew how much he hated having anything put over his head. Then, crouching as he slid, he entered the cloud of smoke. Ben activated the night vision of his breathing mask. Beneath his skis, the snow felt lumpy. He could see four person-shaped figures near the mouth of the tunnel. A moment later he was there too. He felt a tug at his elbow and turned to see Toru beside him, bending to unfasten his bindings, his movements swift and practiced. Ben was fast, but it still took him twice as long.

A single railway track led into the tunnel. Once his skis

and boots were removed, Ben reached into his backpack for the Gemini Force uniform issue safety boots. They were reinforced for impact as well as waterproof and ultra-lightweight. Less than four minutes after leaping out of the helicopter, Ben was ready to enter the tunnel, just behind Toru. A final glance around confirmed that Jasmine was nowhere to be seen. Ben guessed that she'd remained beside the helicopter with her father, to release and prepare the rescue sled that was suspended below the aircraft.

He turned back towards the dark abyss. His ears began to tune into the nightmarish sounds that echoed from its walls. The fiery roar of flames consuming human flesh, plastics in the interior of the cabin, metal and brick, making no distinction. It was all fuel. The sizzle of the spray of high-pressure water that a firefighter was using way up ahead, battling the blaze in the most distant carriage. The billow of steam that mingled with tarry smoke.

But from survivors – nothing. He was enveloped inside stillness – a silence of the worst possible kind.

Rigel stood at Ben's right, waiting, patient and obedient. His fur was clotted with powdery snow, right up to the middle of his torso.

Ben leaned over, vigorously brushing the dog with gloved hands until he was mostly clean. He checked briefly that the radio microphone of Rigel's wearable technology collar was activated. Then he adjusted the dog's breathing apparatus, a specially designed muzzle that encompassed the hi-tech collar and fastened like a harness around his abdomen. Sensors on the collar could be triggered by the dog biting down in specific spots; each one would send a pre-recorded voice response to Ben's radio headset. Even with the night vision of his goggles, Ben knew that in smoke this dense, Rigel had a better chance of locating survivors than any human.

'All right, Rigel.' Ben hummed through his breathing mask, tugging slightly on the dog's harness, bringing the dog to attention. 'People, Rigel! Find, find, FIND!'

With a rough bark that was muffled by his own mask, Rigel disappeared, bounding into the smoke. Ben hurried along until he'd caught up with Toru, whose striding form was lit from behind by the halo of light in the gloom ahead, a dazzling crack in the wall, where the aircraft had plunged into the tunnel.

They'd reached the wreckage. Ben followed Toru into the first carriage. He almost turned around the instant he saw the inside. Even the breathing mask couldn't entirely filter out the acrid, stomach-churning stench of burned human flesh and insides. His eyes closed as, instinctively, he flinched at the sight of a face, blistered and blackened almost to the point where you couldn't make out that it belonged to a person. Nausea surged through Ben, knocked him to his knees. He scrambled to pull the mask aside. Then Ben was vomiting hard, all over the floor of the burned-out cabin, grateful that there was no one to see him.

He staggered to his feet, wiping his mouth with the back of his hand. He rearranged his breathing mask and looked around; keeping his eyes carefully away from the vision that had triggered his vomit reflex. Bodies were heaped over each other. The funicular train ran with most occupants standing. They'd toppled over each other and were now layered at random over the floor of the carriage. Fire fighters had already extinguished the blaze and moved up the train.

Ben doubted that anyone could have survived. Trembling, he pushed through to the second cabin in time to see Toru stooping to grasp the shoulders of a burned body. Ben rushed to grab the same person at the ankles. With surprising delicacy, Toru shifted the body and then two beneath it, until they'd uncovered the final layer of crash victims.

'They're all dead,' Ben said, hearing the disbelief in his own voice.

Toru wiped gloved hands on his jacket. 'In this carriage, I think so. Any word from Rigel?'

Ben felt another tremor go through him. The image of what he'd seen in the previous carriage flashed before his eyes.

There'd been nothing from Rigel – not a peep. He didn't want to think about what that could mean. The train wasn't very long, only three carriages. By now Rigel must have covered all three. They moved along towards the third carriage, but Ben's hopes were dashed when he saw another rescue worker emerging. It was one of the snow-mobile crew, a tall Swiss whose brown hair stuck up behind his breathing mask. He was shaking his head.

'We got three people out before you came,' the Swiss was saying. He spoke Swiss German, a dialect that Ben understood only when he paid close attention to every word. 'I don't think there are going to be any more.'

At that, Ben broke into a jog. He reached the third carriage, which was badly derailed. It had toppled off the line, hit from the opposite end by the nose of the aeroplane. It was leaning against the side of the tunnel so that Ben had to get onto his hands and knees to crawl through the gap that remained. He emerged to see Truby in the fire suit, blasting the train's engine with liquid nitrogen extinguishers in the suit's arm modules. Truby met his gaze with the same grimace he'd seen in the Swiss rescue worker's face.

'*Found someone alive.*'

At the sound of the American-accented vocal recording that Rigel's hi-tech collar had just sent, Ben startled into action. He glanced up and down the flank of the carriage. There was no sign of Rigel.

He began to call for the dog, walking back and forth alongside the blackened containers of all those charred bodies, yelling for Rigel. Still nothing, not a single bark.

'*Found someone alive,*' came the recorded voice again. Somewhere, Rigel had located a breathing survivor. The flat-coated retriever's training allowed him to detect the tiniest traces of a tell-tale scent - chemicals released shortly after death. He must have found a body where these chemicals weren't present.

Exasperated, Ben let out a yell. 'Yes, but where?'

Finally, the dog responded with a bark. The sound came from somewhere further down the tunnel, behind a pall of thick black smoke.

'Hey,' Ben said. But a sudden commotion from behind him had all the other rescue workers distracted.

'There's a survivor,' he heard Toru say, curtly, in his radio headset. He watched as Toru and the other rescuers started to huddle at the crash site, which gaped open around the body of the crashed aeroplane. They'd apparently spotted someone outside.

'But Rigel,' Ben said, then stopped. He wasn't getting

their attention. Rigel wasn't barking any more. Ben began to trudge in the opposite direction, deeper into the tunnel, towards where he'd heard the dog's barking. Within seconds he was wreathed in thick smoke. It was belching out of something up ahead. It wasn't just dark – the smoke was so thick that visibility was practically zero. He slowed, stepped carefully along the rail tracks, to where the smoke was at its most dense. Suddenly, his foot kicked against something solid. Both arms outstretched, he began to feel the outline of a curved structure. Metallic, smooth. He could feel the heat of the surface through heat-resistant gloves, and the soft thwack of Rigel's wagging tail as it swished against his legs. He bent down, fumbling in the darkness for the dog, heartily grateful for the breathing mask.

'Good dog, you found one of the plane's engines! Where's the human, boy? Find find find!'

Rigel responded with a muted yelp, then pulled away. Ben just managed to grab hold of the dog's collar, following him around the jagged, smoking wreckage. There, face down in the snow with both hands over his face, was a man wearing an orange hi-visibility jacket. His legs were trapped beneath the engine.

The man – presumably some kind of railway worker - was absolutely still. It was hard to believe that he was alive. And yet, Rigel wasn't detecting the tell-tale odour of death. Was it possible that the railway worker was alive?

Hurriedly, Ben dropped to his knees beside the man's

head, and began to scoop away the snow that had been pile-driven into a heap around him. When he'd freed the man's hands and head, he carefully placed the man's face on one side. Gently, he inserted two fingers into his mouth to clear his airway. Swiftly, he removed a case containing an Oxyboks self-rescuer from his backpack. It would provide thirty minutes of clean air that could be breathed through a tube – vital to any situation that involved smoke and poisonous fumes. Ben pinched the man's nostrils together as he inserted the end of the breathing tube into the unconscious man's mouth. Then he waited. His desperation increased. The rail worker's legs were probably broken, crushed by the wreckage. Maybe a lot more than broken. The engine must have snapped off from the body of the plane, hurtled through the tunnel, flaming, searing hot; impossible to avoid.

The feeling of his own pulse beating in his neck reminded Ben to check for the man's pulse. Nothing. He gasped in frustration. This wasn't going to work. Even if the man was still breathing, how would they save him? He pressed harder against the man's carotid artery and held his fingers absolutely still. Then he felt it. The faintest throb.

The man was alive. He was pinned beneath the smoking wreckage. He'd probably lost blood – in the blackness swirling around them, Ben couldn't see. One thing was certain - the man had very little time left.

━ APOCALYPTIC ━

Once he'd satisfied himself that the survivor was breathing through the tube, Ben shuffled down to where the man's legs disappeared beneath the curved edge of the bulky engine. He began to dig, his gag reflex almost triggering when he withdrew his hands. Caught in the beam of his headlamp, they were shiny from the viscous blood that coated both gloves.

Ben forced himself to start digging again, loosening the man's legs without touching them.

'A little help down here!' he called into his radio mic. 'I found a survivor. Not a passenger from the train, at least I don't think so. I think he was in the tunnel for some other reason.'

'On my way,' Truby replied.

He heard Truby's approach before he saw the fire suit flying past the burned-out engine. Truby stopped a little beyond and began to walk back. Meanwhile, Ben did his best to free the rail worker's legs. The man's injuries were horrific. But at least the heat seemed to have stemmed the flow of blood. Apart from the first handful of slush and gravel near his legs, the melting snow around him was mostly clean.

The guy would probably lose his legs. He'd have

smoke damage to his lungs. But there was still a chance that he'd live.

'Still bleeding?' Truby asked.

'No,' Ben said. He peered through the smoke at Truby's silhouette. 'No. His wounds are . . .' He suppressed a shudder. 'His wounds are cauterised.'

Truby positioned a shoulder against the wreckage. 'Help me get this off him.'

Ben joined Truby in heaving against the metal. It was still hot, like a recently-boiled kettle. He had to take care not to get his cheek anywhere close to the surface. After a few seconds it began to shift. Then it rolled. With a final shove, they hurled it to the opposite side of the tunnel. Instantly, the smoke cleared and Ben could see that the injured man was regaining consciousness. As he came back to himself, his features twisted in agony.

Truby crouched low, picked up the man in his arms and then straightened up. 'Dammit,' he said after a moment. 'Ben, switch on the jet pack for me, to fifteen percent. The mechanism inside the mask isn't working.'

Ben approached, did as he asked, and said, 'You really need to get that suit fixed.'

'It's experimental,' Truby snapped, above the sudden roar of a concentrated gush of flames from the fire suit's jet. He rose slowly into the air. With the limp form of the survivor in his arms he looked like a metallic angel escorting someone to heaven. Ben watched his graceful flight from the tunnel, and then set about cleaning the blood off his gloves by rubbing both palms between handfuls of un-melted snow.

He could feel the tingle of tears at the corners of his eyes. Mental images of seared, melted flesh persisted stubbornly. A little too roughly, he grabbed Rigel by the scruff of the neck.

'We need to get out of here, boy,' he mumbled. They made their way back to the mouth of the tunnel. Most of the rescue workers had cleared out by now. A few had gathered near the tunnel and were staring down the slope. About a hundred metres below, another rescue worker was climbing upwards, approaching what looked like a snow mogul.

Ben said, to no one in particular, 'Have they found the woman who filmed the crash site?'

The Swiss rescue worker next to him turned. 'Pardon me?'

'The woman with the camera phone – the one who was streaming the video we were watching? The video that got cut off?'

With open curiosity now, the Swiss stared at the insignia of Ben's Gemini Force jacket. 'Gemini Force? There was another guy here a moment ago; a Japanese fellow. He was wearing the same uniform. From where are you coming? The United Nations?'

Ben raised his head just in time to see the slender figure of Jasmine approaching from the diagonal, somewhere above the tunnel. As her skis hit the upwards slope of the tunnel, she arced into an impossibly graceful leap, soaring over the swell of the tunnel and easily clearing the wreckage of the aeroplane.

For a moment, Ben couldn't say a word. Then the Swiss guy made a sound like a garbled groan of disbelief. Gloved hands slapped together. 'Crazy person,' he muttered. 'Skiing in a disaster zone. But what an *artist!*'

Ben just shook his head in wonder. He could see two rescue helicopters now; the Eurocopter piloted by Addison had been joined by a red chopper from the local mountain rescue.

Addison's voice cut through the radio. 'They found a skier who got hit by a wall of snow when the plane crashed. The woman is lucky. My guess is, an air pocket saved her. Most people who get buried in snow aren't breathing after fifteen, twenty minutes.'

'Same with the guy Rigel found,' remarked Ben. 'He'd made an air pocket with his arms. Or else breathing that smoke would have killed him.'

She continued, '*Taurus*, you're gonna have to ski yourself and Rigel back down to Grindelwald. We're on a deadline here. Gotta drop the medical litter off with Jazz so that she can take her survivor down on the sled. Then we're gonna fly the guy that you and Truby brought in to hospital. He's in a bad way.'

'Wilco, *Aquarius*,' answered Ben. 'Just get that guy to safety. I'll see if Jasmine needs help. Although I think I'm gonna be skiing down there the hard way,' he added, eying the obstruction presented by the plane wreckage. There was no way he'd be following Jasmine in vaulting over that.

'Roger that, *Taurus*. See you back at the inn.'

The Eurocopter flew past him, heading down the slope. Somewhere behind the wreckage it paused, hovering. Ben could just see the edge of the medical litter being lowered. A moment later the heli was on its way again.

He was deeply relieved that they'd managed to find the buried skier and the railway worker, although the latter's lack of movement was ominous. Yet, it didn't really feel like a 'good job'. Inside those carriages, Ben had seen at least a hundred dead bodies. One hour before, that tunnel must have been a scene of barely imaginable, apocalyptic horror.

Three survivors on the train, plus one railway worker. And a skier who could be considered as collateral damage.

That was all.

⏤ FANBOY ⏤

Ben tried to sound cheerful. 'That was an *epic* bit of skiing.'

He pushed a huge plate of mixed salad across the table to where Jasmine had taken a seat. She'd just been hugged by her father, then Addison and Toru. Truby had looked on in admiration. All of which had kind of made Ben feel a little shy about joining in. He really didn't want to stand in line to hug Jasmine. Not that she didn't deserve the plaudits, but it kind of felt a bit weird. A part of him felt – rather strongly – that he should have been the first to embrace her, to congratulate her. When he couldn't be the first, then it was as though he was just another Jasmine fanboy.

Once, Ben would have been OK with that. But not any longer. Watching everyone hugging Jasmine, he decided it would be best if today, he simply treated her like another crew-mate. She'd done a terrific job, high-fives all round.

Jasmine's skiing. *Amazing.* Ben could imagine exactly what his late mother, Caroline, would have made of Jasmine's skill on the snow. Caroline had prized manners and discretion above many things, but she had never been opposed to steering him towards girls that she thought merited his attention. An athlete, a girl who could hold her own on the slopes, would have Caroline arching her eyebrows in admiration and nodding subtly in encouragement. Jasmine smiled to herself. She didn't return Ben's gaze until she'd drizzled copious amounts of creamy Swiss dressing over her salad. Then she looked at him with an amused expression.

'It was nothing compared to rescuing that rail worker guy, though,' she said, her light brown eyes thoughtful as she ate a forkful of shredded red cabbage. Ben watched in silence. 'Yep,' he said, eventually. 'He was in a bad way.' For a moment, he seemed unable to take his eyes off the way she twirled the fingers of one hand in her dark brown tresses.

'I can see why you do it,' she was saying. 'It could become kind of addictive. And then there's Rigel. I mean, he's amazing, when you think about it. If it wasn't for your doggy, your rail worker guy would still be there, most likely.' She beamed. 'You did a great job training him, Ben.'

He nodded his thanks, and picked up his cutlery. They were seated at a heavy, antique pinewood table on the terrace of a large inn next to the railway station in Grindelwald. Despite the horrific tragedy, the tables were crowded and although the mood was sombre, with little talking above hushed whispers, food and drink continued to flow.

Ben wondered at his own ability to eat, given the horrors he'd seen several hours before, up in the

Jungfraujoch tunnel. But even memories like that couldn't stop his tired muscles needing to regenerate and rehydrate. Just the same, he couldn't bring himself to order anything grilled.

Feeling despondent, Ben picked at his own salad, and speared one half of a hard-boiled egg with his fork. 'I might have to go veggie,' he said, gloomily.

Jasmine grimaced in sympathy. 'Was it really bad?'

Ben nodded, chewing. 'There was almost no way for anyone to survive,' he said. He hesitated. Maybe it would be better not to talk about the details. 'Not unless they got out right at the beginning. The local rescue team picked up most of those people before we arrived. But inside?' He shook his head, gravely. 'Not good. The fire spread right through the carriages. Loads of people were trapped. Because most of them were standing, when the train was hit, they fell over. They must have struggled and stuff, but the heat and the smoke? I want to believe that most of them were dead from smoke inhalation before they started to burn.'

Jasmine didn't answer, and for a moment Ben regretted having told her even that much.

'Let's change the subject,' he said, with a pale attempt at a grin. 'Tell me how you got to be so incredible at skiing.'

Jasmine wrinkled her nose. 'That? It's boring. I skied and skied like there was nothing else in the world.'

'Well, you impressed me,' Ben remarked. 'And you

got down there pretty darn quickly, which none of us could have done.'

'I was just glad to help,' she said. At the other end of the table, Toru, Addison and Dietz were eating steaks, which Ben found baffling. Truby, he noticed, was eating soup.

'Everyone at the hospital was talking about how it happened,' Jasmine told him.

'How? You mean like, what went wrong with the pilot?'

'Nothing, apparently. He's dead, of course. But it looks like the plane was taken over by remote control.'

Ben put down his fork. 'What?' He turned to Truby. 'Is that what they're saying, Jason, that someone jacked into the aeroplane's controls?'

Truby nodded. 'Correct. That is the story that's making the rounds on the newsfeeds.'

'What d'you think?'

'I don't think any sane person flies a plane into a mountain. Especially not when it's into a tunnel filled with conference delegates.'

'Except, y'know, the same lot who did 9/11.'

Truby looked doubtful. 'In Switzerland? Not exactly the home of terrorism, is it? The country is neutral. Although apparently, quite a lot of the world's biggest criminals, including terrorists, bank here.'

'Might it be something to do with that?' Ben asked.

Truby picked up his drink – a lager. The glass was engraved with the local coat of arms and the Swiss flag. 'There might be something to that, Ben,' he said eventually.

They returned to Gemini Force One by night.

Wherever possible, Truby preferred that the various rescue crafts, but especially GF Two, were flown under cover of darkness. Only the small aeroplane that Addison usually piloted, GF Four, was equipped with camouflage technology.

A genuine cylinder of light-bending 'invisibility' could be deployed around the static base, GF One, to make it impossible to see it from most positions except directly overhead. GF Four's tech, however, was all about illusion, about fooling the eye of the beholder. The aeroplane's skin was covered with LED plaques, each one projecting a high-resolution image that made a composite of whatever was directly behind the aeroplane at any given second. A sharp eye could detect GF Four by the strange movement of light in its vicinity, because the image was always at least a millisecond out of sync. But in general, the camouflage worked, unless someone knew to search for the craft.

Ben often found himself wondering how much longer it would be possible to keep Gemini Force a secret. They'd done a few rescues by now, where they'd worked more or less alongside another, local rescue agency. Today, a rescue worker had taken a good look at the emblem on Ben's uniform jacket and had asked a question he'd been asked before. At this point, Ben could still count on the fingers of one hand, the number of people who'd looked him in the eye and asked 'What is Gemini Force?'.

No one who'd asked that question figured quite as starkly as Minos Winter, the British-born mercenary who'd planted a bomb on the deepwater oil platform, Horizon Alpha. In his nightmares, Ben occasionally found himself back in the dark corridors of *PSV-Macondo*, the platform supply vessel in which he'd finally confronted the violent, cunning criminal. He, Addison and Julia Bencke, Gemini Force's Brazilian helicopter pilot, had been lucky to escape with their lives that day.

Ben could see why Jason Truby made so much effort to conceal the existence of Gemini Force. But in a world of phone cameras and the Internet, how long could it continue?

'Just supposing someone does find out about Gemini Force? What then?'

Discreetly, Ben asked Dietz this question during GF Two's three-hour flight back from Switzerland. Dietz took a moment to consider his response. 'I don't know how much you know about Jason's connections in the US defence department, Ben?'

'I've met 'Emma',' Ben replied. 'If that's even her real name.' He remembered a red-haired, rather elegant middle-aged woman who as far as he could tell, was Truby's contact in the US government. Truby had taken him to meet her for the precise purpose of identifying a photograph of Minos Winter. 'She sort of good as told me that she worked for the Department of Defence. Or the CIA, or y'know, one of them. I'm guessing Truby has some kind of deal with those guys, right?'

'They wouldn't sit back and allow advanced aircraft to enter airspace all over the planet without some kind of agreement being in place, that's for sure,' Dietz agreed.

'You think Truby's connections in the military or whatever are good enough to have references to us deleted from the Internet?' Ben asked Dietz. 'Because seriously, right from the first time I found out about

GF One and all, I haven't been able to find a single reference to Gemini Force online. And there kind of really should be, by now. Don't you think?'

'There would be and there have been,' confirmed Dietz. 'You're quite right. Just at the moment various agencies help to keep us off the search engines and out of the news. But there's the invisible web too, the "darknet", the place where all the bad guys hang out. And that part isn't so easily policed.'

'Darknet?' Ben was immediately intrigued.

Dietz made a face, very anxious. 'It's a nasty place, Ben. You don't want to go looking in there.'

'But there are mentions of us, in darknet?'

Reluctantly, Dietz admitted that he'd found several.

'So the secret is out?'

'In the sense that there are now criminal operators who are aware of our existence, yes. That's been the case since Minos Winter. He's only seen three of us with his own eyes; you, Julia and Addison. It's not something that worries me, right now. But yes, Ben, if you're implying that we have to prepare for a day when everything other than our location is common knowledge, then I'd have to agree.'

Ben wanted to talk more, but Jasmine joined them and Dietz immediately turned the conversation to her future.

Later, back on GF One, Ben approached Jasmine at the kitchen station. She was making a grilled sandwich, with slices of Emmental cheese, dill pickles and tomatoes.

When she offered to make one for him too he accepted, saying jokily, 'I like it when you make me food.'

Jasmine handed him the plate without saying anything, then placed her own sandwich carefully on the sideboard and turned to him with her back against the surface, both hands gripping the edge.

'You like it when a girl prepares food for you?' she said, a little coyly. But Ben knew her well enough to detect an undercurrent of annoyance in her voice.

'Oh no,' he said, replacing the sandwich before he'd had a chance to take a bite. 'I'm not having that.'

She smiled sweetly. Too sweetly. 'Having what?'

'You, that,' he said, gesturing with the plate in his hand. 'Making out that I'm some sort of sexist loser, saying that girls are best in the kitchen or whatever.'

The dangerous smile didn't budge. 'But isn't that exactly what you're saying?'

'Huh, no way! Can't a bloke just appreciate a girl – a *person* – for doing a nice thing?'

'Would you say the same thing to Tim?' she said, now allowing the smile to slip. 'Or Paul? Or Toru? Or even Addison, who is an actual girl? I bet there's no way you'd say it to Addison.'

'Whaaat?'

'It worries me,' Jasmine said, frowning slightly, 'because before, when we were setting out to the mountain, to the Eiger, you said you didn't think I should be involved in the rescue, that I should stay in the chopper.'

'Only because I didn't want you getting hurt,' Ben blurted.

'I see. You thought the weak little girl should stay behind and what – make sandwiches for the brave rescuers?'

Utterly bewildered, Ben felt himself growing warm with indignation. 'When have I ever implied that you are anything but fully awesome and one heck of a skier?'

'You pretty much have to accept that last part, since I was offered a place on the Swiss Olympic ski cross team. It's when it comes to the idea of me being an actual useful part of Gemini Force that you have a problem.'

Ben put his plate down with a thud. 'No,' he said, struggling to keep his voice even. He could see, out of the corner of his eye, that Toru was strolling past about five metres away. He'd cocked his head towards them and had definitely slowed his pace. 'No, I have never implied that. And if I have, well . . .'

Then he stopped. Because he'd stumbled ahead into territory that he hadn't taken the time to map out. She'd practically ambushed him. Ben was beginning to see where this could lead and it wasn't good. He wasn't ready for this. Not yet.

'If you have? Which you have, by the way,' Jasmine said, folding her arms, 'just FYI.'

Ben lowered his gaze for a second, unable to meet her eyes. 'If I have,' he continued, unsteadily, 'it's only because I worry. About you. Not because I don't think you can do stuff,' he said, rushing the last sentence out before she could jump in with an objection. 'I know you can do stuff.'

And finally, he raised his gaze to meet hers, voice trembling slightly as he said, 'But because I like you. So much.'

Jasmine's jaw dropped a little and she steadied herself with one hand on the sideboard. 'You . . . you *like* me?'

Ben nodded. 'Yeah,' he breathed.

Jasmine gulped. All her confidence seemed to have drained away. 'I . . . I guess I like you, too.'

His eyes widened. 'Really?'

She nodded. 'Uh huh. I think, I think I like you a lot. When you're not being a sexist loser.'

'Oh, come on,' he murmured, softly. 'You don't really believe that. Do you? My mother was Caroline Carrington. One of the most awesome women ever. One of my best friends is Addison Nicole Dyer, ditto that. I've just given away all my mum's money to be managed by a thirteen-year-old, totally amazing girl in South Africa. And right now, the person that I like more than anyone else in the world just happens to be a girl. I'm definitely a ladies' man.'

'A ladies' man?' she said, teasingly, pulling at Ben's sleeve. 'Does that mean that all the ladies like you? Or that you like them?'

'It means he's spending precious time chatting to girls when he should be attending a meeting,' said a voice from the other side of the kitchen preparation area.

Ben looked past Jasmine, who spun around to see

James Winch. The geological engineer was calmly making a cup of coffee behind them. He couldn't have been there too long. Hopefully James hadn't heard the whole, rather cringe-worthy, exchange.

'Truby wants to go over all the imagery from the inside of the tunnel. Ben, your helmet cams were videoing the whole time, obviously. He wants to do full playback and get your recollections while they're still fresh.'

'Now?' Ben said in disbelief, with a glance at his watch. 'It's after ten!'

'I hate to interrupt such a tender scene,' James said. His sly smile made it actually impossible for Ben to look at Jasmine. 'But Jason Truby can be very insistent. And memories about an event like that fade faster than you think.'

Ben gave a quick nod in response. There was no point arguing. He threw Jasmine a brief, helpless look. To his relief, she responded with a friendly smile.

'I'm going to bed anyway. It's been such a day.'

'All right.' He left with James, with one final, longing gaze at Jasmine. It wasn't how he wanted to leave things, by any means.

— PTSD —

Addison stuck her head around the door to Ben's cabin. He glared at her from where he sat on his bed. Dressed only in a wrinkled T-shirt and boxers, he was sewing a button back onto a blue-and-white checked shirt. 'Hey there,' she said, grinning. 'I noticed you skipped the gym.'

'Didn't skip,' grumbled Ben, pushing the needle through the button. 'I just decided to go a bit later. Truby said we could have the day off. I'm having a lie-in, not that it's any of your beeswax.'

'I'll go with you later to the gym, buddy. If you haul ass right now, I'll throw in a helicopter lesson.' Primly, she added, 'When you're done with your needlepoint, of course.'

'It's my favourite shirt,' Ben said, a touch defensively.

She lifted a hand to cover her mouth, but he still caught the smile. 'Who doesn't love a guy who knows how to sew?'

'It's an important survival skill,' he said, tersely. 'Didn't you ever see *Rambo*?'

'Sure I did, meathead. So – what's the decision about that heli lesson?'

Ben hesitated. It was difficult for Truby, Julia or

Addison to find time to give him a real-life helicopter lesson, and he'd had enough of simulator programs. Added to the fact that he'd kind-of-sort-of already flown a helicopter solo, less than a month ago, Ben did feel that the time had come to get moving with qualifying as a helicopter pilot.

On the other hand – *Jasmine*. He'd barely slept for thinking about her.

What did she mean by saying that she liked him too? Did she properly *like* him? What about her boyfriend, Jonah? She hadn't mentioned him once since they'd picked her up from Collège du Léman. But last time Ben had seen Jasmine, when they'd gone to a Rock Snakes of Mars gig in Dietz's hometown, Jonah and Jasmine had still been an item. Ben pretended to be all civilised and everything, kept a respectful distance. But what he really wanted was to prise Jasmine away from this Jonah guy. At the first sign that she was anything but thrilled with Jonah, Ben should make some kind of move.

It was so much easier to *plan* than to *do*.

A real, live girlfriend. It was faintly ridiculous to have reached sixteen and never had one – at least that's how Ben felt. The truth was that he simply hadn't met a girl that made him feel the way Jasmine did. He'd never spent enough time around girls, hardly any day-to-day stuff at all, just fancy parties where the girls looked so impossibly grown-up that they made him feel like some awkward kid.

Jasmine was honest and direct and brave. And really cute. She looked him right in the eye and made him get serious about who he really was and what he really wanted. He should have been the same way with her, Ben realised. Should have accepted that maybe Jasmine would one day express a wish to join Gemini Force. She had just as much right to it as he did, after all.

He'd spent a lot of the night thinking about that. Wondering how he might have done things differently. Every time, however, he came up against the same problem.

It made Ben feel physically sick to imagine Jasmine in some of the situations he'd experienced. Struggling to avoid being thrown off a sinking yacht, clutching at the railing whilst stormy waves battered the deck. Trying to escape from a huge, burning and capsized oil platform, surrounded by floating corpses, bloated and charred, just as horribly as the poor people he'd seen yesterday. The people in those train carriages, on the mountain.

Ben blinked and closed the thought down, instantly. It was still far too raw. His mind wanted to run very far away from any thought of what he'd seen in the Jungfraujoch tunnel. Having to go through those images with Truby last night had been hell. If he hadn't had thoughts of Jasmine to look forward to, to absorb him as he tried to sleep, Ben very much doubted that he'd have slept at all.

When Ben didn't reply immediately to Addison's invitation, she swung on the door for a moment, and then stepped right in, plonking herself down into one of the two chairs, less than half a metre from his bed. She paused for a moment and her expression changed, without warning. The lazy grin and easy attitude vanished. Instead he saw a hint of anxiety, but most of all, caution. 'Rough night, huh?'

Ben slid both legs out from under his duvet and onto the floor. He gave her a querulous glance and disappeared into the tiny shower cubicle behind the partition that hid the bathroom area of his cabin. When he didn't hear her leaving, Ben called out, 'You're sticking around then, are you?'

'I want to talk to you about yesterday,' Addison replied. Ben stilled. He could hear that she'd moved to stand just outside the shower, probably leaning against the partition.

Huh. She really did want to talk.

'Yesterday?' he repeated. She couldn't mean about Jasmine. The only person who had a clue was James Winch. And if James Winch – of all people - was a gossip then there was no hope. It would mean that there could be no secrets, no private life, on GF One. Bad enough for the adults, but a total disaster for Ben, who would have to live his whole life in front of their eyes, all his firsts and failures as well as any triumphs.

For an only child like Ben, the thought of this appealed to him almost as much as it *appalled* him.

'Um, OK,' he said. '*What* about yesterday?'

Addison made a squawking sound. 'Uh – about all the

nightmarish things you saw inside that tunnel! I mean, that's a case of Post Traumatic Stress Disorder waiting to happen, right there. Don't you think you maybe need some help with processing that?'

Ben was silent for a moment, just concentrating on rinsing the shampoo out of his short, light brown hair. 'Processing that', as Addison put it, would mean talking about it. Talking about it would mean thinking about it.

'Nope. No, I don't think I do.' He turned the water off and with one hand, reached for the towel that hung from a railing behind the partition. When he faced Addison again, the towel was tightly wrapped around his waist. 'I'd like to get dressed now. Could you clear off?'

Exasperated Addison blew through puffed-out cheeks. 'Kid, whatever you want. I just need you to know that I'm here for you, whenever you want to talk. You're not alone in having seen stuff like that. And just FYI, Truby's kinda regretting letting you get so far into that tunnel. He didn't expect it would be that bad. Toru's getting a whole stormageddon from Jason about how he should have gone ahead and stopped you once he saw how bad it was and . . .' Addison shrugged. 'Anyways, it's a hot mess. You get the picture, I'm sure?'

Ben pulled a plain blue T-shirt over his head. 'If JT was so bothered about me seeing a pile of burned corpses then why did he force me to go through the photos with him?'

'That's part of what made him so mad. He had to

get a second look through that stuff with people who'd actually been in there. You know, for forensic reasons.'

'It's not fair to blame Toru. I had no idea that JT might want me to stay out.'

'He didn't communicate that too well,' Addison agreed.

Ben though for a moment. 'So – he actually wanted to hold me back?'

Addison nodded. 'Sure. Just the same way that you didn't want Jasmine to go there. You want to know what JT said to me, when we were flying back over in *Leo*?'

'Go on.'

'He said that he sometimes forgets how young you are. Forgets that you aren't quite like the rest of us, that you've never served in the military. That you've never been to war.'

'Maybe not,' Ben said, defensively. 'But I've, you know, I've done a lot of pretty hard core *stuff* with Gemini Force.'

'No doubt, no doubt.' Addison nodded. 'Well then, you feeling in the mood to fly the Sikorsky?'

Ben placed both hands at the small of her back and gently ushered Addison out of his cabin. 'Geddout,' he muttered.

Once she was outside, he finished dressing, took a few fingers full of hair wax from a tub of product and rubbed it between his hands, warming it. Then he smeared it into his hair, checked in the mirror that he looked vaguely presentable, and joined Addison outside.

'Making yourself pretty for Jasmine?' she said, with a wicked grin.

Ben froze. 'What have you heard?'

Addison's eyebrows darted upwards. 'Not a thing. But *now* I'm sure as heck going to try and find out!'

'Don't put your hand in there.'

The voice was behind him, and it sounded trustworthy. Familiar yet not. Who was speaking? Ben wasn't even sure if the voice was male or female.

'Don't put your hand in there. It's a black hole of pain.'

Ben stared at the train carriage before him. Red paintwork was bubbling on the door. Very strange. He reached out to touch it. The door opened and he toppled inside, arm first.

The heat began in his fingertips. It rapidly spread to his shoulder. He was aware of a wave of agony sweeping through him. Pain, literally licking its way up his arm. When it reached his shoulder it was so overwhelming that he opened his mouth to scream. And couldn't. The scream died in his throat. The pain seemed to reach his head and he almost blacked out. Barely able to breathe now, Ben gazed in frozen horror at his arm. It was turning black in front of his eyes. Crisping flesh, roasting and melting. Pain roared in his ears, blocking out every sound.

'What did I tell you?' said the voice again, this time sadly. 'It's a black hole of pain.'

Ben jerked upright, slamming the crown of his head into the bunk above. He stifled a yell, right arm clutching instantly at his left elbow. The pain was still there, itching and burning. He blinked and looked around, holding his left elbow in a pincer-like grip as it continued to throb. He was in his cabin, fully dressed. Had obviously fallen asleep that way. He struggled to remember why he was asleep fully clothed. It took him a full minute to remember that he'd gone back to his cabin after lunch, intending to watch some YouTube videos.

Shakily, he released a breath he hadn't even realised he was holding.

If I was dreaming then why am I still in agony?

He stared, dumbfounded, at his left arm. It prickled and stung beneath the vicious grip of his own right hand. Yet there wasn't a scratch on him.

I'm still dreaming, still dreaming.

He willed it to stop hurting, urging himself to relax. Directed peaceful, soothing thoughts at the hot tingles in his arm. Ben closed his eyes, then opened them. He let out a single, broken sob of relief when he realised that the pain had completely gone.

He rose, unsteadily, to his feet. His tablet computer fell to the floor. He'd been using it to watch videos made by Holden White, the lead singer of Rock Snakes of Mars. With a trembling hand, he replaced it on his bunk. He began to tune in to the sounds of the base. Quiet voices close by, in the corridor outside the crew quarters. More distantly, strident voices involved in what sounded like a robust discussion. The low, ever-present hum of the engines that kept Gemini Force One powered and balanced under the Caribbean Sea. The occasional purr of sea-water pumping through the ballast sections, the whirr of water jets.

Ben stepped into the corridor, strode past James Winch and Julia Bencke. They were engaged in a quiet conversation. One look from Julia was enough to tell Ben that they hadn't expected anyone to be in the quarters at this hour. Then he noticed James's hand, lightly touching Julia's upper arm.

Oh.

Immediately, Ben lowered his eyes. He mumbled a quick 'hullo' before backing away. The pain in his arm was forgotten as he made his way to the chintzy lounge area, where he knew Jasmine would be, with Rigel. She'd begged to take his dog for a walk around the base – a task of mind-numbing dullness for Ben. Luckily for Rigel, Jasmine was on the base so rarely that she didn't mind the prospect of walking the length and breadth of every staircase and walkway.

Ben was dying to tell her that he'd seen Julia and James together, possibly stumbled on a romantic moment between the two. But by the time he dropped himself next to Jasmine on the paisley-patterned two-seater sofa, Ben had already realised that this probably wasn't a great idea. After all, if Ben expected Winch to keep quiet about seeing *him* with Jasmine, he couldn't exactly behave like a blabbermouth.

'Hey,' she said, with a gentle smile.

'I just had this really horrible dream,' Ben said. 'My arm was burning. It was unbelievably painful. I mean, *actually*. And I didn't even know I was dreaming. I even dreamed that I'd woken up. And I was still in pain. Still in the dream.'

Her eyes widened in sympathy. 'Oh that's horrible! It must be because of what you saw in the tunnel.'

Ben looked at her for a moment. The train, the burning. His arm turning black in front of him. Just thinking about it now made him retch enough to make his eyes water and his cheeks sting with embarrassment.

Jasmine reached for him with both hands. She held Ben at the elbows, steadying him. 'Ben! You've gone white as milk!'

Helplessly, he stared down at her. Before he could think about what he was doing, he'd knocked her hands away. 'Sorry,' he whispered, uselessly, a moment later, when he saw her shrink back. To distract himself, Ben fixed his gaze on Rigel. The dog lay curled up, contentedly snoring on an oval, maroon-coloured rug.

'I think maybe you should see Dr Nina,' Jasmine said, anxiously.

Ben swallowed, feeling awkward. 'Yes. Probably.'

'Addison was worried that something like this would happen,' she added.

He nodded, unable to meet her eyes. 'I guess,' he

managed to say. For some reason, Ben kept wishing that he'd wake up and find that this, too, was a dream.

Then he felt her fingers on his arm, found himself staring at her nails. They were neatly filed and varnished with a pale, almost translucent pink polish. Jasmine didn't move her hand. When Ben finally wrenched his eyes away, he forced himself to look at her face. The expression he found there almost stopped his heart.

Jasmine was gazing right into him. There was a look of such tender concern, the way she'd looked at him when his mother had died. This time, however, there was definitely something else too. A kind of *yearning*.

Her attention kept flickering to his lips. Ben was suddenly aware of how dry they were. He sucked in his lower lip, moistening it. He could hear the unevenness of her breathing, could feel the beat of his own heart. He leaned a little closer, tentative, giving her space and time to move away. But she didn't. Then he decided to throw all caution aside. Ben leaned in and touched his lips to Jasmine's. The kiss was over in seconds, little more than a taste of what he really wanted. He pulled away with reluctance, and threw a quick glance over his shoulder. As he'd feared, far across the deck, Tim and Paul hastily turned away. They'd probably been watching, most likely slack-jawed.

Jasmine touched her fingers to his cheek. 'What's wrong?'

'You have a boyfriend,' Ben muttered, every syllable an effort.

Her hand dropped down to rest lightly on his shoulder. She looked down for a moment, unsure of herself. Then she brought her gaze up once more to meet his. Ben found he was having to use all his concentration to keep himself in place, unmoving. Part of him wanted to just get out of there, away from curious eyes, away from the feelings that Jasmine was stirring up inside him, and from what that awful dream could mean.

Yet, another part of him wanted to just pull Jasmine against him and properly kiss her. And to hell with 'that Jonah kid'.

'Jonah,' Jasmine said, hesitantly, 'is . . . he's . . . Let me take care of Jonah, all right? I'm not married to him. I can still kiss you.'

On the sofa, Ben straightened up. 'If I was your boyfriend, I wouldn't want you kissing anyone else.'

'If you were my boyfriend,' returned Jasmine, 'then maybe I wouldn't *want* to kiss someone else.'

Ben could hardly breathe. 'What . . . what are you saying?'

Jasmine smiled, shyly. She reached for him and then stopped herself when she noticed Ben tilting his head in warning, towards Tim and Paul. Instead, she settled for resting an elbow on his shoulder and running a hand through his hair.

'Silly boy,' she said and chuckled, twisting a strand between two fingers. Ben leaned into her touch, couldn't stop himself. He smiled in response, a daft, goofy grin, because he didn't know what else to do.

━ FIRST CLASS ━

'Truby wants to see you.'

The first few times that this comment was thrown across the main deck, Ben pretended not to hear. It sounded casual, so he treated it casually. But the truth was, he really didn't want to face Truby.

The previous night, Ben, Dietz, Toru and Truby had examined photos of the Jungfrau tunnel disaster together. Ben felt sure that he'd given a good account of himself. He'd watched, unflinching, as image after image, each more horrific than the last, flashed on the screen. In each case, they'd been looking at something else in the photograph – they'd been looking past the dead bodies, burned and twisted, at some structural aspect of the railway carriage, or at the pattern of bodies. It was amazing, the kind of picture you could assemble even after the fact of an incident like that. But for once, Ben couldn't sustain any interest in the forensic piecing together of clues.

He'd walked out of that room with his head held high, hadn't allowed Dietz or Truby to have any idea how much the last hour had affected him. A good night's sleep, he was sure, and it would start to be behind him.

But apparently not.

Jasmine had urged Ben to talk to Dr Nina Atalas, who was Gemini Force's chief of medicine and also a qualified psycho-dynamic therapist. Ben had agreed, mainly because he couldn't face an argument - not with Jasmine. Yet he didn't want to talk to Nina, either. It wasn't only that he feared reliving what he'd experienced in that tunnel. There was more at stake. What if Truby decided that this was a sign that the work of Gemini Force was damaging Ben?

What if Truby put Ben's entire career with the rescue agency on hold?

Addison said that everyone on the team had gone through bad stuff. Maybe so, thought Ben. But they weren't children. Technically, he still wasn't an adult.

Ben suspected two things. One: if his mother were still alive, she wouldn't have let him go solo on some rescues, the way he had. And two: Jason Truby felt a powerful sense of duty to the memory of Caroline Brandis-Carrington. If he thought that Ben wasn't coping, he'd intervene to protect him.

'Is there something wrong with your hearing, laddie?'

Ben glanced up from the sofa to see Tim Hardy standing over him. The young Scot, Gemini Force's submarine pilot, was regarding him with impatience.

'OK,' muttered Ben, standing up. He leaned down to stroke Rigel's head. 'I'm on my way.'

He headed to Truby's quarters, found the door open, and no one inside. He went directly to the tiny, two-person elevator that stood in place of the usual shower cubicle. Ben took the elevator down to Truby's private suite, of which he'd only ever seen the main office.

The suite was flush to the outside of the base, with porthole windows looking right out into the blue of the ocean. The muted lighting, unique, twelve-sided grey brick design of its walls and the various photographs, spacecraft blueprints and newspaper clippings gave the room the atmosphere of an ultramodern museum to Jason Truby's exploits.

Ben hadn't been in the room for several weeks. There'd been only one change since then and he noticed it immediately. When Truby saw where Ben was looking, he nodded, once. 'It's a great photo,' he murmured.

With only a quick glance to acknowledge the comment, Ben strode over to the desk, where Truby stood. Before he could reach for the frame that now sat on Truby's desk, the man picked it up and handed it to Ben. After he'd examined the image for a moment, Ben returned the framed photo of Caroline Brandis-Carrington to Truby.

'It really is. Mum would like that you picked it.'

Truby replaced the photo on the desk. 'Good,' he replied, almost formally. 'I'm glad you think so.'

There was a brief, uncomfortable pause. 'Umm,' Ben said. 'What's the news from Switzerland? Any leads on the terrorist incident?'

'We may have a motive,' Truby said. Ben was surprised at his casual reply. Truby typed something into his computer and then angled the screen so that Ben could see it better. 'That's the value of the Swiss franc today. Against the Euro.'

'1.85?' Ben struggled to follow Truby's reasoning.

'It was closer to 1 when we were there. That's almost a one hundred percent devaluation in just a few days. If someone had bet hard against the Swiss franc – and people almost never do – they could have made a serious amount of money.'

Ben could only gape at him in horror. 'You think that's why someone killed all those people – to devalue the Swiss franc?'

'I think it would be very hard to prove.' Pensively, Truby folded his arms. 'Benedict, how'd you like to take a trip with me? I think maybe we could both use a few days away from the rescue business.'

'When?'

'We'd leave later today. It might be an idea to return to Switzerland, see if we can ask a few questions.'

Ben's thoughts went straight to Jasmine. She wasn't leaving for another two days. He'd miss precious time with her.

'It would be you, me, and Jasmine,' Truby concluded. 'You'd be joining me at the World Economic Forum in Davos. Naturally, we'd first return Jasmine to her school in Geneva.'

Well, at least that put his worry about missing Jasmine to rest.

'A conference? What would I do?'

Truby chuckled. 'Not just any conference, Ben. It's *Davos*! The world's leading thinkers in finance and economics and a host of other issues of immense importance to just about the whole world. I've been invited almost every year since Trubycom made the list of global top ten companies.'

Ben suppressed a frown. Obviously, to Truby this didn't sound like a giant snooze. But Ben couldn't see anything interesting about hanging out with some massively important 'thinkers' and economists and assorted business leaders. He'd had his fill of people like that when he'd travelled the world as the son of Casper Carrington, the hotel millionaire. His father had made his fortune in knowing how to please such folk.

'Sounds *fascinating*,' he mumbled.

Truby guffawed. 'That wasn't too convincing,' he said. 'But you should still come. We get to stay in a very fancy hotel. Lots of great food and drink. Great skiing.' His smile faded. 'And you need the break,' he said, more gently. 'You need to get away from . . .' At this, Truby stalled. For a moment, Ben thought he saw Truby's eyes turn dark with caution, or even worry. 'From your work,' the man concluded.

Ben shuffled, uncomfortably. He paced over to the wall, pretending to examine a framed blueprint diagram of GF Two. 'All right,' he agreed, after a moment. It wasn't like he had a lot of choice. He'd do anything, at this point, to stop Truby from asking any probing questions about how he was 'processing' the Jungfraujoch tunnel disaster.

If Truby honestly didn't realise how sick the thought made Ben, the idea of returning to the country where all that had happened, to snow and mountains and to skiing, then Ben certainly wasn't going to put him straight.

At least he'd be able to spend some quality time with Jasmine on the trip across the Atlantic.

'Good,' Truby said, decisively. 'That's settled.' He sat back down in the high-backed, leather swivel chair on the other side of the desk, and waved a hand at Ben, dismissing him. 'We'll be hopping across to Cancun International at around seven. So that gives you a couple of hours to pack. Don't worry about food. We'll grab dinner at the airport.' He flashed his teeth in a sudden, broad grin. 'If you like, you can be the one to tell Jasmine that we're flying first class. Oh and Ben, try to make that sound as exciting as it is, especially to someone who hasn't done it before.'

'I don't know what you're on about,' Ben said, allowing a touch of his sullen mood to infect his voice. 'I've hardly ever flown first class. My dad was a bankrupt, remember? All his money was in the hotel business. He used to boast about it, in fact. Said that first class was for losers who had money to burn. We went business class, at best.'

'Is that what you think of me?' Truby's eyes twinkled, a little ominously.

'Course not,' Ben sighed. 'Are you kidding? This, Gemini Force? It's off the hook. This is what I call "money well spent".'

'How about flying first class? After all, you are a Count, *nicht wahr, Herr Graf Carrington-Brandis*?'

For a moment, they faced each other in silence as Ben tried to work out if Truby was just teasing him, or testing him.

'You need to learn, Ben, that there are always going to be people who have a problem with how other people spend their money. Don't let it stop you doing the right thing. And once in a while, sure, treat yourself to a luxury. A lot of people have jobs that rely on folks with a lot of cash, like me, spending it, buying goods and services that keep people in work. Especially in Switzerland, and for that matter, in Austria. Remember the real crime, with money, is not to spend it well.'

Ben forced himself to nod. 'It'll be cool to fly first class,' he said, as enthusiastically as he could. But leaving Truby's underwater suite, Ben was choking out the words, thinking of Zula and all the kids in the tiny village of Harambe, the ones whose parents lived underground for months at a time, trying to scrape a living by scraping the walls of abandoned gold mine shafts.

The price of a first class transatlantic ticket, just one, could feed, clothe and house a kid like that for more than a year.

HOTEL LE DAUPHIN

'Davos is nothing special,' announced Jasmine, when Ben told her. 'Better to stay in Klosters. It's prettier, it's all chalet style. Like Grindelwald.'

Ben gritted his teeth. Did no one, not even Jasmine, get that he didn't ever want to go back to Grindelwald? 'We're staying in some really fancy hotel though,' he said. 'Le Dauphin.'

Her eyes sparkled. 'Ah well then, that's different. Hotel le Dauphin is super-nice. You'll fit right in there, Count Benedict.'

He groaned. 'Not you too.'

'What?'

'Giving it all the "Count Benedict" treatment.'

Jasmine's smile widened and with the flat of one hand she pressed him, gently, into the back of the taxi that had picked them up from Geneva Airport. 'You ask a lot, Herr von Brandis.'

'Seriously, drop it.'

She leaned against him and gave him a peck on the cheek, saying sweetly, 'Whatever you say, Ben.'

Ben could tell that Truby was watching them from the front passenger seat, through the driver's mirror. When the car arrived at Collège du Léman, Truby allowed the driver to open the door for Jasmine. Before Ben could follow her out of the car, Truby tapped him on the shoulder saying, 'I'm gonna let you do this alone, kiddo.'

Nodding, Ben escorted Jasmine down the long path to the main entrance to the high school. It must have been lesson time because there were no students to be seen, only a steady hum of low noise from inside the nearby classrooms.

She faced him with her hands at her side, one clutching the strap of her rucksack. At no point did she reach for Ben. When, tentatively, he bent to kiss her goodbye, Jasmine turned a cheek to him. After a brief hesitation, Ben pressed a kiss there, then to her other cheek.

'*Au revoir*,' he said, a little ruefully.

'*Auf wiedersehen*,' she said. And now, after a quick glance around to make sure that no one was watching, Jasmine squeezed his hand. 'Next time I see you, the boyfriend issue will be resolved, I promise you.'

Ben nodded. 'Good to know.'

She took a step backwards. 'Goodbye, then.'

'Bye.'

He watched her disappear into the school, an expression of helpless regret on her face. When Ben returned to the car, Truby was waiting in the back seat.

'What – no kiss?'

Ben glanced to the side so that Truby wouldn't see his cheeks flush, and made a point of shrugging. 'She didn't want to. She was afraid someone might see us.

Her boyfriend goes to this school,' he said, adding, 'her current boyfriend.'

Truby chuckled. 'All right, Ben! I'm glad to see you happy about a girl. All work and no play makes Jack pretty darn boring.'

'What about the guys on GF One?'

'What guys? Which ones?'

'No one in particular,' Ben said, hastily, thinking of Julia and James. 'I just meant like, in principle. Are people allowed to hook up?'

'You mean like Toru and Gary Lincoln?' Truby shrugged. 'I didn't put a stop to them, so I can't exactly do anything if anyone else gets together. However, Toru's been pretty unhappy since Gary died. And that's made me wonder about sending him into missions, definitely. If team members are in relationships, it does double the chances of one of my crew being vulnerable to that.'

'To what?' Ben said, bluntly. 'To having their partner killed in action?' He regretted his words instantly, and flashed a quick look at Truby to see if he'd reacted. 'I'm sorry,' he mumbled, the words falling from his lips in a reflective apology. The last thing he'd meant to do was remind Truby – and himself – of Caroline's death. Then Ben realised that he'd also implied that his mother and Truby were more than just friends, and he had to turn his face away again so that Truby wouldn't notice his appalled expression.

Kill me now, please.

Truby didn't answer, only shrugged. 'No need. We all live so close together. In some ways, it's inevitable that these bonds will form.'

'Maybe we should expand?'

To this, Truby just chuckled. 'Hold your horses, mister. I'm only just adjusting to having a crew of eleven. Plus one dog.'

'But we aren't at capacity yet. There's still no *Aries*.'

During the drive to Davos, they debated the issue of the empty seat at the zodiac-themed conference table at GF One. It wasn't an easy decision to make, according to Truby. Gemini Force's final person would have to complete the team, plug any remaining weaknesses and bring some new skills to the group.

Ben couldn't help wondering if Truby was thinking that he'd prefer to recruit a pair of friends who'd already worked together, as he had with almost every post up until now. Including Ben's mother, who'd joined alongside Addison. If Ben failed to make the cut at the end of the year, then Truby would have two places to offer.

Perhaps he was waiting for that?

It was dusk by the time they arrived in Davos. Hotel le Dauphin shone against the backdrop of black woods and snow; a giant, cream-coloured fairytale castle of a building, with small turrets at two corners of its five-storey structure. In front, a queue of black and white limousines were waiting to drop off their passengers.

'What the heck is this?' Truby muttered. The taxi

driver turned and spoke in a French-inflected accent. 'Security checks, Mister Truby. The terrorist attack at the Jungfraujoch has raised the threat level. No one can enter the hotel without the checks being made.'

Watching Truby, Ben saw a flash of the man's rare, burning anger. A muscle twitched in his jaw for a moment before Truby said, 'We'll see about that.'

When their car joined the line, Truby jumped out and had removed their luggage from the boot before the driver could object. Truby tipped him with a twenty franc note and signalled to Ben that they should leave.

'It's all going to be lines on the ski slopes,' he muttered. 'I'm not making a line to get into the hotel.'

Nor did he. By a process that Ben guessed had to do with Jason Truby's extremely well-known face, they were speedily escorted to a suite on the top floor, with an unobstructed view of the mountains.

'Not too shabby, is it?' Truby said, smiling. He took two bottles from the mini bar; an India Pale Ale and a Coca-Cola, which he handed to Ben. 'Drink up. The World Economic Forum is picking up the tab.'

They unpacked and dressed, Truby in tan slacks, a plain white shirt and a dark blue blazer, Ben in red jeans, white T-shirt and a charcoal-grey tailored jacket. Then they left the room, ready to hit the cocktail party that signalled the first event of the conference.

Hotel Le Dauphin was itself hosting the welcome party in its new, modish underground bar, part of which sloped upwards to the surface, where it opened to the night sky. Wall to ceiling and wraparound glass carved out a circular structure at one end of the bar. Ben and Truby strolled into the bar to the sounds of animated chatter and the pulse of electronic dance music.

Ben looked around in mild surprise. He'd expected to see a bunch of grey men and women in grey suits, sipping fizzy white wine. Instead, however, it was a cool-looking crowd, as eclectically-dressed and vibrant as he'd ever seen. No one was wearing a suit, only stylishly coordinated trousers, jeans or cords with jackets. Most of the young people, in their twenties and thirties, were total stunners, especially the women, Ben couldn't help but notice. Their clothes looked expensive yet understated. There were quite a few people, men and women, who looked much older, maybe forties, fifties and sixties. It was this group that seemed the most relaxed, surrounded by little huddles of younger, better-looking people.

Truby noticed Ben watching the room. He passed him a tall glass of lager, beaded with moisture from the cold. Every now and then someone would wave at Truby, call out in recognition, and Truby would wave back, but then guide Ben further into the crowd. They kept going until they'd reached a vantage point from which they could oversee the entire room.

Truby released his grip on Ben's elbow and raised the Martini glass that held his own Manhattan cocktail. 'Cheers, Benedict. To your first time at Davos.'

Ben clinked his glass and sipped the lager.

Truby said, 'So, what d'you think?'

'It's more glamorous than I expected. I didn't rate economists for being so well-dressed.'

Truby laughed. 'Most of these folk aren't anything to do with the conference. They're more like hangers-on. Media types who like to mooch about close to the centres of power and influence.'

'There's a lot of that here, is there?' Ben said, doubtfully.

'Oh, yeah. For example, two o'clock. That's Jed Maddox, brother of POTUS. He's talking to Regina Powell, the US Secretary of Defense. And that very cute blonde making all the jokes, by the look of it, is the movie star, Karen Lohn.'

'I thought she looked familiar,' marvelled Ben. 'And yet weirdly out of place.'

'Over by the bronze pillar we have someone I thought you'd be sure to recognise.'

Ben focused, then gasped. 'You're right. That's *thingy*, who was arrested for selling government secrets to that newspaper!'

'Right, Marcus Clarin. He's supposed to be getting extradited, but a bunch of celebrities keep bailing him out, paying for another team of lawyers to fight an appeal.'

As Ben's eyes hovered close to the infamous former computer specialist, he noticed a flurry of excitement. Following the ripple of glasses raised to the latest arrival in the bar, Ben's mouth fell open when he saw who it was.

'No way. That's Holden White, from Rock Snakes of Mars! What the heck is Holden White doing here?'

'You didn't hear about his "sabbatical"?'

White, a skinny, bleached-blond teenage rock star was sporting a wholly new and rather austere haircut, no longer dreadlocked and floppy but short; tidy and sculpted in a razor-sharp line precisely one inch from the base of his neck and matching a new, equally bleached goatee beard. Ben eventually tore his attention away from him and peered at Truby. 'Sabbatical?'

'As of this year, Holden White is taking time out from being a rock god to promote his book, his YouTube channel and his support of a new global movement. The WFW – World for the World.' Truby pursed his lips. 'You're a teenager; how do you not know this?'

'I'm working bloody hard for Gemini Force, is why not!' Ben stuttered. 'How do *you* have time to know this stuff?'

'I have a guy at Trubycom whose sole job is to keep me informed, every single day, about which parts of our planetary insanity I should be paying attention to.'

'Gotta say, Holden White is pretty awesome,' said Ben, noting the clutch of beautiful women who surrounded his favourite rock star.

Truby sipped his Manhattan and said, thoughtfully, 'He certainly seems to think so.'

➤ HOLDEN WHITE ◄

It took less time than Ben had expected to get to the front of the cluster of bodies that had crystallised around Holden White. Yet again, Jason Truby's fame preceded him.

At the centre of his crowd, the singer stood in a louche, relaxed manner, one elbow lightly resting on the shoulder of a gorgeous brunette girl who didn't look much older than Ben. She was gazing up at Holden, who seemed oblivious to her presence as he held forth to the gathered company. There was absolute adoration in her eyes. White must have looked up for a moment and caught a glimpse of Truby and Ben looking down at him from the raised dais on which they stood.

'Y'all right, Astro Boy?' he roared out, loud enough to quell the chatter in his immediate vicinity. Everyone turned to stare at Truby.

Truby smiled mirthlessly and raised his glass high. 'Hey yourself, Guitar Boy.'

'I'm the front man,' growled Holden White. 'Not a bleedin' guitarist.' He was pushing his way through the assembled crowd now, ignoring the hurt glances of those whose conversations he'd abandoned, mid-sentence.

Ben started to move, but Truby grabbed his wrist.

'Stay here,' he said, his voice suddenly edged with steel. 'Make him come to us.' When Ben glanced at Truby, the grin was still plastered all over his face.

White reached them a few seconds later. 'Well look at us,' he said in a rapid-fire, clipped Manchester accent, offering a fist to Truby, who bumped knuckles with the singer as though they were old pals. White reached back under his white dinner jacket and stuck both hands in the pockets of his black leather trousers. A white dinner shirt completed his outfit, open, untucked and worn with an unfastened black bow-tie. He looked like he'd already been at a party this evening. 'What are we like, eh? A multi-billionaire computer genius and a rock star knockin' about with a bunch of politicos and number crunchers, all ruminating on global destiny and whatever. Effin' brilliant, or what?'

White turned his attention to Ben and nodded. 'All right, pal? You Truby the Younger or some'at?'

'He's Benedict Carrington,' Truby said, before Ben could reply.

'We nearly met last summer, in Abu Dhabi,' Ben said, when Holden White's face registered a total blank. 'The Snakes were going to play at the opening of a hotel. I was there with my mother. But there was an accident, during the air display, so . . .'

'Yeah yeah yeah, and we got cancelled. You're that kid, aren't you? Hotel Carrington's lad.' White's attitude had completely shifted. He pulled his hands free and reached out with one to shake Ben's hand, which he did with surprising vigour. 'Mate, you were *proper* mental out there. I mean it. Total respect, man.'

Ben found himself grinning. 'Thanks. It looked harder than it was. I mean, my mum and me were both pretty experienced climbers.'

'In't he modest?' White said, with a glance at Truby. 'So, Jason Truby, I can imagine what *you're* doin' 'ere. No doubt hoping to connive your way into some massively important decision that's going to influence the telecoms industry, eh? Make sure you get your own way for Trubycom? But what about the lad? You just an 'anger on, Benedict Carrington?' he asked Ben, enunciating every syllable of his name. 'Or you got any actual purpose?'

'Probably more of a "hanger-on", if I'm honest,' Ben said, with a bashful smile. 'Here for the skiing and to meet interesting people.'

White gave him a wicked grin. 'Nowt wrong with that, mate, I'm here for a bit o' that myself. Lot of really top birds here. Or blokes, liking blokes is fine too. Some of them are pretty enough to be girls.'

'I've kind of already got a girlfriend,' Ben admitted.

Holden White nodded. 'Course you have, good-looking boy like yourself, not short of a couple of quid, neither.'

'I'm . . . I'm not rich any more,' Ben said, and then suddenly regretted saying anything. As he buried his face in his drink for a moment, Ben felt his cheeks almost sizzle against the chill of the glass. It was ridiculous how excited he was to be meeting one of his favourite rock musicians. He felt giddy and slightly out of control.

'You what? You give your money away or some'at?'

'I used it all to set up this charity in South Africa,' Ben confessed. He kind of didn't want to go into details but on the other hand, he did. It felt amazing to be talking to Holden White about this. Holden White had famously spent months living rough before he'd been discovered on YouTube, busking, when he was sixteen. He'd been poverty-stricken after the breakdown of his family and his mother's suicide. Social issues had formed the bedrock of the singer's work outside of the Rock Snakes of Mars.

'Yeah, but you didn't give it *all* away.'

Ben nodded, while Truby merely allowed himself a quizzical smile. 'Oh – he did. Every cent. But Mr White, you should know that Ben's a huge fan. Aren't you, Ben? He specifically requested that his father ask for you at the opening of the Sky High Hotel.'

'And I went to see you guys play in Bern in December,' Ben said, breathless enough that he had to take care not to stumble over his words.

Holden White's eyebrows disappeared into his carefully flopped fringe of white-blond hair. 'Serious? That's mint, that is. You're all right, Ben.'

Ben had to press his lips together hard not to emit a giggle or some other pathetic sound of glee, which was all that was rushing through his veins in that moment.

The Rock Snakes of Mars had risen from relative

obscurity a year ago, when True Fans like Ben had been downloading their songs online, and watching live streams of their concerts in their home town of Manchester. Then something had happened. Holden White's video blog, in which he posted videos about the song-writing process, his love life, but most of all his passion for social justice, had somehow gone viral. The band's third CD album, 'XLV', was produced by one of the biggest music labels in the business, with a huge world tour to promote the Snakes. Their appearance at the Sky High Hotel, booked before they hit the big time, would have happened just as it was all starting to take off for the band.

Ben couldn't help thinking how odd life could be. Things often worked out in ways you would never have imagined. It had been a wild thrill to be involved in the rescue at the top of the Sky High Hotel. The idea of his mother's rescue agency had been born from that act. She'd met Jason Truby. At the time, the only downside had been the fact that Ben had missed out on meeting the Rock Snakes of Mars. Now here he was, hanging out with Holden White himself.

White turned his attention to Truby. 'So, is the Astro Boy going on the VIP trip tomorrow?'

'Probably,' Truby replied. He didn't react to the second use of White's silly nickname for him, but Ben knew Truby well enough to know that only politeness held him back. There couldn't be many people in the world that could call him that and get away with it.

There couldn't be many people who'd even dare try, Ben realised.

But Holden White wasn't just anyone. He was the lead singer of one of the biggest rock bands in the world. His political views had won him an invitation to speak on behalf of the youth of the world, at the World Economic Forum. All this – and he was still only nineteen years old.

Holden White simply nodded. 'You an' all, Ben?'

'I don't know,' Ben said, with a glance at Truby. He'd heard nothing about the trip. But Truby had that manner – he'd often leave it to the last minute to reveal his plans. Ben had started to wonder if this was because Truby liked to keep everyone on their toes around him, always alert and ready for the unexpected. As far as Ben was concerned, it was working.

Truby's jaw was set hard as he answered. 'There's a trip for some of the delegates. We're going to visit a new museum, it's up in the mountains, has its own lift and ski run. There's an art exhibition, and a restaurant that's already earned a Michelin star. They're going to unveil what's thought to be a genuine Van Gogh, a never-seen-before painting that's been languishing in someone's safe deposit box for decades until they tracked down the heirs. You'd be very welcome to join me, Ben.'

'Paid for by bankers,' White said, with a nod that was too proud, too approving, to be sincere. 'Nice of 'em, don't you reckon? Putting a bit of all that cash back to share culture with the plebs. What d'you say, Ben? You fancy it? Or would you rather knock about with me?'

Ben's fingers went slack briefly, almost letting the glass slip through his fingers. A whole day with the lead singer from his favourite rock band?

'No' was not an option.

➤ THE NO-SHOW ➤

'Holden wants me to go speed riding, y'know, paraskiing, where you fly with a parasail, but with skis. Tomorrow morning, at seven thirty. With him,' Ben said between long strides as he kept pace with Truby along the corridor. 'How cool is that? Speed riding with Holden White!'

'Forgive me if I find that rather unlikely,' Truby replied. He'd been offhand on the subject of Holden White from the beginning of the evening. But in the past half hour, the same chilly attitude had infected his conversations with Ben, too.

'Why not? I've done parasailing before,' Ben said. 'More than once. And I'm a good, safe skier. I can probably manage to bend my knees to lift skis out of the way of the odd obstacle if I have to.'

'I suspect there's more to it than that.'

'Yeah, sure. It's mainly in the control of the parasail, actually. Which I already know how to do.'

Truby drew to an abrupt stop, still several metres from the door to their hotel suite. 'I'm not doubting your ability, Ben. I'm doubting that singer's.'

In private, Ben had also wondered, fleetingly, if Holden White hadn't bitten off more than he could chew. They'd been talking about winter sports in the bar, sometime after Truby had wandered off and left them to it. Holden White had mentioned how he'd seen some skiers with parasails reaching the bottom of a slope and almost falling into the road in front of his limousine. Ben had laughed and said that yes, it often happened, because those *speed riders* (as they preferred to be known), didn't exactly follow the rules of the piste. 'You have to go with a guide,' he'd said. 'And you pretty much have to end up on the road or very near to it because otherwise you're stuck in the mountains, miles from anywhere.'

Holden had mentioned that he'd like to try it, and Ben had been more than willing to join him. But still – he was surprised and impressed to hear that White was a good enough skier to try such a dangerous sport. Somehow Ben imagined that White's upbringing hadn't been the sort that included ski lessons. But White had flat-out contradicted him and laughed, 'It's not that difficult. I picked it up on a couple of holidays with the band.'

Ben's eyes had widened, the only sign of scepticism he'd shown. He himself had often watched speed riders taking off from the wild end of a mountain, the side that only the best skiers would dare to descend. The sport looked amazing but also, pretty scary. Only now, after months of hard physical training and more than a few tricky situations could Ben seriously contemplate trying something so risky.

In bed that night, still buzzing too much to sleep, he downloaded some detailed instructions on parasailing and speed riding to his smartphone and studied them thoroughly, until he knew in detail the structure and function of every part of the parasail. At which point Ben felt pretty confident to try the sport, as long as they went down with a guide.

Holden White had to be either seriously brave, or seriously reckless.

Either way, Ben wanted to be there to find out.

The next morning he woke at around six-thirty in the morning to find Truby already up and dressed, seated at the round dining table in the living room section of the hotel suite, tablet computer in one hand and coffee cup in the other. Around his neck was a jersey-silk scarf, gun-metal grey with an electric blue trim.

Ben found his eyes drawn to the scarf. It looked exactly like one his mother had bought for him in an airport once, when he'd forgotten his.

The memory caught him off-guard like a punch to the stomach.

'What's up?' asked Truby.

Ben took a seat, still dressed in the shorts and T-shirt in which he'd slept. He helped himself to scrambled eggs, bacon and two pancakes from the plates that had been set out by room service. 'Your scarf. Mum gave me one just like it. I think I left it at school, annoyingly enough.'

Truby stared for a moment, then unwound it from

his own neck and handed the scarf to Ben. 'Here. It's yours.'

'Hey . . . I didn't mean to take your scarf.'

'It's fine, I can get another,' Truby said. 'Take it. It reminds you of Caroline – I want you to have it.' He added, 'Who knows, maybe we bought the scarves in the same airport store?'

Ben was about to make some non-committal conversation opener when he noticed that Truby's eyes had narrowed. Ben wrapped the scarf loosely around his throat, then picked up a fork. 'Is something wrong?'

'I've been reading a report about the attack on the Jungfraujoch tunnel. It's kind of incredible but they think they have a lead on who might have remote-controlled that plane.'

'Oh. Was it Al Qaeda? Or, y'know, one of the new versions of it? Was it ISIS?'

Truby looked confused. 'What? No! I already told you – what would Middle-Eastern terrorists be doing in Switzerland? Switzerland is neutral. No one attacks Switzerland.'

'Maybe it's personal? Like, maybe someone they wanted to kill was on the train?'

'But why kill all the innocent people too? Trust me, Ben, if you want someone dead and you can afford to pay, it's not so difficult to get results. No – from the very beginning I've had the feeling that whoever did this is someone new. And *new* is bad. It's real, real bad.

New means that no one in the world's security services has any clue about how to stop it happening again.'

'But you said they have a lead?'

Truby nodded. 'Yes. That's the surprising part.'

'OK so what does it say? And who wrote it?'

Truby opened his mouth to answer when on the table in front of him, Ben's mobile phone began to buzz. The screen lit up with the words 'Holden White'. Ben was reaching for the vibrating phone before he'd even started to say, 'Hang on, I'm just gonna take this call from Holden.'

Ben turned away so that Truby wouldn't see the way excitement overtook him when he pressed the 'answer' button. It was too late to get his breath under control too, so when he actually spoke to Holden, his words came out embarrassingly garbled.

'Huh – hey hey, Holden White, what's going on?'

'Hey hey yourself, Count Ben,' replied Holden after a brief pause. 'Well – I'm flat on me back, feeling like I've 'ad a rough night in the Northern Quarter.'

'Oh,' Ben said, deflated. 'So we're not going speed riding then?'

There was a snickering laugh. 'You what? I don't give up that easy, matey-boy. You think I'd ever get anything done if I let a bit of a hangover blight my day? I've got responsibilities, man. Course I'm going. What about yourself?'

'Hell yeah,' Ben said, relief surging through him. 'I'm so up for this, you've no idea.'

They arranged to meet thirty minutes later, in the lobby. Ben turned back to his breakfast and began to shovel eggs and bacon into his mouth. Truby was already on the other side of the room, putting on a dark brown sports jacket over his blue plaid shirt. He slid the tablet computer into the inside pocket and then checked his mobile phone.

'You were saying?' said Ben, his words muffled through chewing.

'It's OK, it can wait. You've got a thing and I've got a thing.'

'Oh that's right, the big VIP trip.'

Truby grimaced. 'Unlikely that I'm going to make that, as things are turning out. I have to go to a meeting with a few guys from NATO to talk about airspace treaty violations. Pity too, because just about everyone important in business, banking and politics is going to be on that VIP trip. The security is insane. I heard that they're making every delegate go through the full body X-ray.'

'That's just ridiculous.'

'It's highly disrespectful, is what it is. One more reason not to be disappointed that I'm gonna be the only no-show.'

Ben thought for a moment. 'Does NATO have an issue with airspace treaty stuff that involves Gemini Force?'

For a moment, Truby considered. He'd finished getting all his stuff together for the day, it seemed, and was on his way out. 'Let's just say that it's an ongoing discussion.'

'I thought you'd cleared it with them.'

'Indeed. But that was before a bunch of wingnuts started remote-controlling jet aeroplanes to fly nose-first into tunnels packed with pharmaceutical conference delegates.'

'I get your point,' Ben agreed. 'Oh well. Neither of us gets to hobnob with the Very Important People. Can't say I'm all that bothered.'

Truby closed the door behind him, chuckling.

➤ SPEED RIDER ➤

'All righty,' said Konrad, a lean, rangy, Swiss ski instructor who was easily thirty-five years old. He looked at the sky. It was a hazy blue, the sun's early morning brilliance obscured by a vast sheet of gauze-like cloud in at least half of the sky. 'Weather outlook - good. Visibility is close to perfect. The snow – deep. We've had some monster falls in the past few days. You probably noticed it in town – they've been working around the clock to clear huge piles from the roads, and roofs too. There's a lot of powder. I mean – a lot. Anticipate that when you touch the snow – take care not to get trapped. Use your sail to lift you out of danger, and never leave it too late, OK?' Konrad breathed out in a burst of heavy puffs, blowing up a balloon of condensed air, then grinned, playfully. 'And cold? Sure; always it's cold in January. But it's bearable.'

Konrad reminded Ben of James Winch, a man who exuded physical confidence, with weathered features that indicated a life outdoors. His hair was dirty blond and streaked with grey as well as the butter-yellow remnants of his most recent visit to the salon for highlighting. His trim, muscular frame was covered in the simple, red one-piece ski suit worn by mountain instructors in the area. A prominent Swiss flag appeared on the right upper arm. 'You're both strong intermediate-level skiers, right?' he said, addressing first Holden White and then Ben. Both nodded, firmly.

'Took to the slopes like a baby to bathwater,' White said, with a lazy grin.

But Konrad frowned. 'This is no joke. There will be times when you don't get the flight right. I need to know that you can avoid an approaching rock or else this ride will be the last one you make on this earth.'

'Chill, man,' growled White. 'I've signed the consent forms like you asked, so's Ben. We're all right.'

After a moment's piercing glance at White, Konrad continued. 'The kit. Your bindings – we're using alpine touring bindings. You've used them before?' He waited for both to confirm before continuing. 'OK, so you know how to free your ankles so that you can use your speed bar stirrup when you're flying. Now – ski poles. We're using the telescoping kind. They'll fold into three sections. Keep them in your backpack during flight. Finally, you'll need a pair of ski safety straps. That way there's less chance of losing a ski while you're airborne.'

With the palm of one hand, White smoothed back his silver-yellow fringe. He examined the kit that had been laid out on a pine table in the hotel's boot room. Ben did the same, then placed all items into the backpack that had been provided. It would fit beneath the pack that contained their parasails.

Konrad drove them to the gondola station for the

nearby Weissfluh mountain, where they met up with Justus, the second instructor. One would fly ahead of Ben and White, the other would follow behind. All four would stay in contact by radio headsets, which Ben noticed were not dissimilar to the ones that Gemini Force used. They rode the gondola along with dozens of other ski tourists, the metal-grid floors of the cable car clattering with the sounds of forty or more heavy boots and skis. Once they'd reached the top of the mountain Konrad led them away from the main pistes and ski lifts, to an isolated area behind the restaurant.

The slope they'd be tackling was spread out before them. It was wide, curved like an immense bowl at least eighty metres wide. Entirely off-piste, the snow was deep in some areas, with moguls and trails that had evidently been carved by snowboarders. Ben could still see a couple of them on the slope below. When he looked at Konrad, the instructor was helping White to unfold the canopy of his parasail and lay it out neatly on the snow, with the skirt and risers totally free of worrisome tangles that might stop the adventure before they even got off the ground.

Ben began to do the same. He'd taken a short course in parasailing in the summer when he'd turned fifteen, and had spent at least an hour the previous night re-familiarising himself with the structure of a parasail and how to arrange it for launch. Taking off with skis on your feet, however, and skiing parts of the mountain on the descent, that would be entirely new. He allowed himself a quiet smile when the instructor checked the red-and-white candy-striped canopy of his parasail laid out on the snow and gave him the thumbs up.

White pulled a ski helmet over his head; gunmetal grey and with a GoPro camera strapped on the front. 'Totally gonna video this,' he said, with a wide grin. 'First time speed riding!'

Ben put on his own ski goggles, and then his helmet, zipped up his jacket and did a last minute check that he could quickly access all his gear. The three of them got into position, ready to launch. Just before Konrad gave the OK for Justus to lift off, White leaned right over in his skis and reached out to bump fists with Ben. Hiding his delight behind a smirk, Ben did the same, barely able to touch the rock star's fist from where he'd positioned his skis.

'Best of luck mate,' Holden White said, tipping his forehead, almost a salute.

Ben grinned back. In that moment they weren't a globally recognised rock star and his fan, they were just two guys on a mountain; excited, apprehensive, eager for a new and exhilarating experience.

He watched Justus take off first. The man pushed forward slightly on his skis until the suspension lines pulled tight enough to lift the canopy from where it lay on the snow behind him. In another second he was floating off the ground, a metre, then swooping away, swiftly rising to a height of five metres off the slope.

White went next. He eased himself into the air with

little more than a nudge of his knees to slide down the slope. Ben went next. The recent skiing experience with Gemini Force had warmed up his ski-legs, so he felt utterly secure. But it was still a major rush to feel himself rising off the snow and floating into the air. Once the initial burst of excitement had washed through him, Ben concentrated on controlling the risers, tilting the canopy experimentally this way and that, just to get a feel of the strength of the air currents. Ahead, he could see Justus and White doing the same thing.

'Very nice,' came Konrad's voice in Ben's radio headset. 'Ben, I'm about ten seconds behind you. We're going to follow Justus down the mountain. For now, try to follow him exactly. Move for move. He's going to announce his manoeuvre, talk through it, and then you do the same thing, OK, about ten seconds later. I'll be behind you, I'll spot if you seem to be making a mistake and I will advise a correction. You got that? Instructions are from Justus, corrections are from Konrad. Or as I like to say, *the front goes to heaven and the back goes to hell.*' The instructor's laugh rumbled in Ben's ears.

Ben took a moment to take in the expanse of white before him, the gentle slopes giving way to harsh, limestone outcroppings that poked out from under the snow once in a while. Further below, from one end of his field of vision to the other, the entire mountain range stretched out, a sea of craggy peaks blanketed in pure white.

'Prepare for the drop-off,' Konrad murmured in a low

tone, suitably awed by the sight that met them when all four wafted over the first major ridge to find themselves soaring thirty metres from the nearest slope.

'That's insane, man!' yelled White into his radio mike. 'Wooooo! Ben-flyboy-Carrington and Holden-mental-White! What a buzz, eh?'

Ben only grinned and steadied his hand on his riser, listening to Justus give instructions for their first major right-handed turn, which led them through a narrow crevasse. Below he spotted a few skiers navigating the better-covered areas. They were moving slowly. Ben guessed that the powder had to be very deep this high and off-piste.

'We're going to rise now,' said Justus. 'Heading for that ridge on the left. When we go over it, get ready to scream for joy. Because you're going to see all Davos laid out, far, far below.'

White just roared with delighted laughter. A knot tightened in Ben's stomach as he contemplated the moment when they'd finally soar to their highest point. They'd feel like gods. Invincible and wise, floating above the ground-bound; absolute masters of the air.

The mountain trailed beneath his skis, the ridge approached. It was higher than Ben had guessed, and at one point his skis actually made contact with the ground, until he heard Konrad yelling, 'Up, up, pull hard, Ben, as high as you can go – and pull your knees up NOW!'

Ben obeyed, instantly, but still, the base of both skis dragged through about half a metre of snow just at the top of the ridge. He felt the left side of his canopy drag. Then before he knew it, Ben was in a chaotic left-handed spin, rushing over the vertiginous lip of the slope and then straight towards a steep slope, a sheer wall of striated grey limestone.

There was a deafening roar, a thunder in his ears. He felt his breath stalling, knuckles white on the handles of the risers, gulping in air as he tried to ask for instructions. But the instructions never came. Instead, all Ben could hear was a fearsome rumble. Freezing cold air slapped the bare skin of his cheekbones, causing his eyes to water. Shock threatened to still his hands completely, but at the sight of his own rapidly approaching doom, Ben managed to yank himself into a corkscrew turn, spiralling clear of the wall and out of danger.

Yet still, his head was full of that terrible roar. Ben blinked a few times to clear the tears. He wobbled in the air as he swung his head around, searching for the other three riders, whose voices had suddenly gone quiet. Then he spotted them, around fifty metres below and to the right.

He looked past them and suddenly understood. The roaring. It wasn't just in his head; wasn't just the panicked beating of his heart.

Beyond the other three riders, a cloud of powder had risen into the air. It moved with ominous deliberation. Lower down the slope, he could see vast stacks of snow simply crumbling away.

'That's an avalanche,' Konrad finally managed to get out, his voice breaking as he shouted into his radio mike. And then louder, in genuine panic, 'Avalanche! Avalanche!'

⟵ AVALANCHE ⟶

The shock caught Ben straight in the guts. It gripped hold of his insides and twisted them until he felt his heart hammering without mercy. His hands quivered at the sight of the mountain falling apart beneath him.

Chaotic currents circulated, they rose up, high enough to catch the speed riders in their draught. He saw it first with Justus, whose bright yellow canopy jerked abruptly into a right-handed helix. The instructor's body seemed to sag for an instant, as though he were being dragged helplessly through the air behind the parasail. But after only seconds he regained control and took a flight path that brought him soaring up again, crossing less than three metres in front of Ben as he lunged to the left.

Then the same updraught seized Ben. His arms tensed with the effort of resisting, he held onto the risers in a vain attempt to avoid being scooped up by the current. It was useless – the air was just too strong. The canopy yanked at his fingers through the risers. Then he was careening down and to the right, almost vertical, with nothing but a ballooning powder cloud and crumbling blue ice visible beneath his feet.

There was no sound in his head but the terrible thunder of falling snow. The urge to screw up his eyes was overwhelming. It was a mesmerising spectacle – white energy rushing towards the nestling town below. After three of the longest seconds of his life, Ben began to hear Konrad's voice screaming in his ear, yelling precise instructions. He barely had time to process them before he allowed his muscles to obey. And like a miracle, his parasail flipped around to the left, he sailed up the airstream and was suddenly following Justus towards a safer part of the mountain.

Konrad's voice crackled over the radio, 'Good-good-good.' Ben craned his neck over his right shoulder to see that both Holden White and Konrad were behind. They'd made neat turns, by the look of things, which hadn't taken them down quite as far as either Justus or Ben.

Their route flashed across part of a ski trail, shaped like a natural half-pipe and edged at both sides with tall fir trees. Two seconds later they'd reached another drop-off. As Ben zipped over the edge he caught sight of two skiers who seemed to have stalled on a ledge.

'We gotta go back,' Holden White began to shout into his radio mic. 'There's two skiers stranded up there!'

'Can't go back,' Justus replied, tersely.

'We have to!' White insisted. 'There's no way out for them!'

'We'll get down and alert mountain rescue,' Konrad said. 'Right now I'm responsible for the two of you. And I'm gonna get you down safely.'

There was a tiny pause. Ben risked a quick look

up, through the gap in his canopy and risers. To his amazement, White was steering himself into a steep climb.

Ben could hear the disbelief in Konrad's voice. 'White, you're out of your mind!'

'Don't I flippin' know it! Follow me, man!' White's voice sang out. 'Let's go get 'em!'

There was an answering growl from Konrad. Then, 'Ben, you follow Justus. Get down, stay out of this, OK?' Then, silence.

Ben glanced up again, took his attention off his own flight path for less than two seconds. Konrad was following White, high into the air, from where they could approach the ledge on which the two skiers were trapped.

Ben's eyes returned to the yellow canopy lower down the mountain. What did they think they were going to do?

'These parasails can carry two, at a push,' Justus was saying. 'Nothing fancy, but they'll be able to take them down to where it's safe.' He added sternly, 'Now, you, keep your eyes on me, yes?'

For a moment Ben felt rebellious muscles tensing up, ready to disregard Konrad's order and join White. A wave of despondency followed, crashing over his desire to join in with a rescue. He was barely able to fly the parasail for himself. If he took a passenger, he'd risk killing them both.

He stalled. Maybe he could go along as a wingman?

But if something happened to him, then Konrad and White wouldn't be able to save the stranded skiers as well as Ben. He might even endanger them. He peered through the mist of powder-snow at White, who soared gracefully beneath his sail. Incredible. The singer was *crushing* it.

Justus's voice buzzed in his ears. 'Ben? Are you ready to follow me down?'

Gulping down chunks of icy air, Ben came back to himself enough to remember that Justus needed a vocal response. 'Yeah . . . yeah,' he managed to say. The canopy of his parasail was pulling him this way and that; his skis were dangling at the end of legs that felt faintly numb and useless with shock. Ben felt his fingers close around the risers and he concentrated. Blanked out the clouds of snow just below that were rolling towards the town of Davos, already obscuring the small lake at the base of the Weissfluh mountain.

'Could it actually hit the town?' he yelled into the radio mic. Sudden alarm at what might result from this avalanche momentarily over-rode Ben's unsteady nerves.

'Not too likely,' Justus shouted back, over the roar of the falling ice and snow. 'The town is protected by avalanche defences.'

Ben knew what avalanche defences were. During summer, the slopes above major towns, big resorts and especially a convention centre like Davos, could be seen to be decorated with a series of terrace-like structures. When the snowfall arrived, these terraces would stack the snow in manageable packets. The kind of snow that caused avalanches, hard compressed snow on the side of a mountain, was protected from a fracturing of the top layer that could lead to a downward flow of huge volumes of the white stuff.

Davos should definitely be OK. Yet as he bobbed high above the roiling white powder below, Ben found it impossible to believe that the town would emerge entirely unscathed.

Someone was going to get hurt. And this time, Gemini Force was thousands of kilometres away. He and Truby would be forced to stand by, nothing more than useless spectators. At this, a stark image of the inside of the burned-out railway carriage bloomed inside Ben's memory. He felt short of breath, for a minute losing sight of the valley below as his mind filled with the nauseating images of charred bodies.

Before he knew it, Ben's fingers were twisting in the riser and the left edge of his canopy was dragging, pulling him once again into a steep left-handed turn. The shock of the sudden drop bolted through him, a tight pain in his chest and guts. He blinked hard, trying to clear the horrific thoughts from his mind. His heart rate was rocketing. Through the thrumming of his own pulse he could just hear Justus screaming, 'Ben, what the hell?'

As he struggled once again to focus on the instructor's carefully-worded guidance, Ben could sense a blush of deep shame working its way through him. He was making this descent unnecessarily difficult, clutching at his risers all the way down, throwing a complete wobbly. A pathetic show – even if it was his first time. Just because there was a bit of an avalanche.

He didn't even manage to land on two feet, but toppled to his left almost as soon as his skis hit the snow. The canopy completed Ben's disgrace by dragging him along for a few metres as it trailed through the deep powder. When Ben made it up onto his feet, he joined Justus in gazing up at the slope of the Weissfluh. The powder cloud was curling round like a river, thundering towards the town. The leading edge had to have reached the streets of Davos by now.

Justus flashed him a friendly, relieved grin. He punched Ben lightly on the shoulder. 'Hey kid, pretty good going. I thought you'd lost it a bit a couple of times, but I have to say, you certainly took control again. I think this could really be your sport.'

'What would you have done?' Ben mumbled, battling to remove his helmet. His hands were trembling almost uncontrollably

'Huh?' Justus didn't seem to follow.

'If I *had* lost it? What then?'

'Oh, you mean . . .' Justus gestured with a finger across his throat. 'If you really lost it?'

Ben nodded. To avoid having to return the man's scrutiny, he pretended to be studying the mountain hard, trying to locate Konrad and Holden White amongst the shadows on the snow.

'Well I'd go catch you. I'm good in the air – very good. I'd try to catch you and fly you down. But if you were too much out of control . . .' Justus grimaced, shaking his head. 'That's why we usually only take people out who've done speed riding before.'

'Holden hardly has,' Ben pointed out. 'And just look at him!'

He'd found the two stray speed riders now – they were floating down, rather fast, with two skiers dangling under each canopy.

Justus broke into a wide, tooth-filled grin. 'Holden White has done this sport before,' he said, confidently. 'He's done it a *lot*.'

'What?'

'I was sure from the moment he took off. Oh boy. He literally stepped onto the air. Newbies don't do that.'

'You're right,' Ben said, after a moment. It seemed obvious now that Justus mentioned it, but somehow, Ben had been duped by White's play-acting. 'Huh,' he added, unable to disguise his bitterness. 'He certainly made *me* look like a total muppet.'

Laughing now, Justus nodded. 'I guess our friend must really want to impress you.'

'No idea why,' Ben muttered. 'It's not like there isn't already enough to be impressed about.'

But Justus's abrupt silencing motion cut him off mid-sentence. The instructor's expression turned flat and then grim as he listened to something over his own radio receiver, which obviously had other frequencies as well as the one over which they'd been communicating in the air.

'What is it?' Ben asked, when Justus finally lowered his hand.

'There's a problem,' Justus said, curtly. 'The guy who paid for this session, Jason Truby, did he take that trip with the VIPs?'

'*Jason* paid for this? Not Holden?'

'No, Mister Truby insisted. Did he go on that trip, Ben? I'm sure he was important enough to be invited.'

Ben shook his head, unsure. 'I . . . I don't think so. He said something about a meeting.'

Justus seemed about to relax, until a sudden fear struck Ben. 'I mean, unless he changed his mind . . . why?'

'Let's hope he didn't change his mind. Because those coaches with the VIPs, they were right under the path of part of the avalanche. And now they've lost contact. They're *gone*.'

⏤ BURIED ⏤

There was no sign of Jason Truby in the hotel suite. Ben stripped off his skin-tight one-piece ski suit and threw the sweat-soaked undershirt into the laundry bag. He showered quickly and dressed in olive-green moleskin jeans, white T-shirt and a blue cashmere sweater. When he picked up his phone to try calling Truby once again, he saw a text from Jasmine flash up on the screen.

Hey is everything ok? They're saying on the Internet that Davos has been hit really bad by avalanche.

Ben's fingers danced across the screen as he typed a reply:

Pretty bad at the edge of town. Some surrounding roads blocked. Worst thing is that two tour buses packed with VIPs have gone missing.

He waited a few seconds for Jasmine's reply.

SRSLY? Is Jason with them?

Hope not. He isn't answering texts or calls. But he said he wasn't going.

There was a longer pause. Then,

You OK? I miss you.

Without hesitation, Ben replied.

Miss you too. Just had a major buzz doing speed riding.

Sounds amazing! Always wanted to try. OK lesson gotta go. xoxox

Ben tucked his phone into the back pocket of his jeans. He was perched on the cream-coloured sofa in the living room area of the suite, opposite the hotel telephone that he'd placed on the coffee table before him. The receptionist had sworn to call him the moment any of the staff located Truby. Ben stared at the phone, willed it to ring.

When after a while it didn't, he began to fidget. He stood up, put on his North Face mountain jacket, warm hiking boots, and prepared to go outside. Maybe Truby was trying to help clear snow? The streets of Davos were pretty badly clogged – Konrad, Justus and Holden White had been forced to return to the hotel via a roundabout route. Still no reply on the phone.

Ben began to rummage through the hotel suite's courtesy package that had been left on a white wicker tray. There was pretty much everything – a shoe shine set, soaps and lotion, a comprehensively-equipped sewing kit, a polythene bag containing squares of four varieties of Cailler chocolate, matches, a scented candle in a shot glass, samples of cologne. After just a moment's consideration, Ben took the lot and stuffed the pockets of his ski jacket with the contents. Things like that shouldn't be wasted. Maybe he'd find someone, even in a town as rich as Davos, who could make use of this stuff.

His hand was on the door handle when the hotel phone rang.

'Ben. You've heard what happened?'

Ben breathed a quick sigh of relief. 'Yeah.'

'Good job we cut that tour, huh?' Truby's voice sounded crisp, business-like.

'Definitely. Where are you?'

'In the lobby. Come down and meet me. I've had quite the start to the day.'

Ben nodded. 'Me too.'

'Oh yes, I heard. Speed riders to the rescue.'

A scowl touched the edges of his mouth. Ben still wasn't over the fact that Holden had been the rescuer; that he hadn't even been able to help. 'That was Holden and Konrad.'

'Impressive.'

'Yup.'

'He's quite the accomplished fellow, Mr Holden White. Rock star, political activist, extreme sports guru, wannabe rescuer. What next?'

Ben turned away. He was a bit sickened by how bad he felt. A better person would surely be pleased to find that his hero had this extra dimension. Yet all it did was make Ben feel comparatively useless. First his nerves had been shredded by what he'd seen inside that horrific train tunnel. Now this. What if he'd permanently lost his mojo?

'There's always someone with something to prove,' he said between gritted teeth, remembering the Austrian boy who'd provoked him in the gym.

In the hotel's lobby bar they ordered a second breakfast of chocolate croissants and coffee, then watched television. Two HD screens were broadcasting the twenty-four-hour news channels, playing in German on one screen, and English in their section of the bar.

The rumours were true, it seemed. The VIP bus tour had set off about ten minutes before the avalanche had started. By the time they'd reached the narrow, tightly curving road that rose to the newly installed art museum on a nearby peak, the avalanche was in full flow. It had struck in two main areas – one was directly above Davos on the Weissfluh. This was the one Ben had witnessed in action. The second had taken place off the beaten track and had initially attracted far less attention. Until people realised that they'd heard nothing from the two luxury coaches, each carrying twenty of the world's most influential financiers, businessmen and even a few senior politicians and their guests. Then the world's media, already trained on Davos for the World Economic Forum, had turned the lenses of their cameras onto macro-zoom.

'I was talking to Dietz when the news began to come in,' Truby told Ben. He used a serrated knife to slice the large wedges of croissant into bite-size chunks which he then lifted whole to his mouth. 'The nationalities of the folk who rented the aeroplane that crashed into the Jungfraujoch tunnel had just been released to the secret services around the world.'

Ben left his coffee untouched where it sat, instead just staring at Truby. 'The secret services,' he said eventually, as evenly as he could. 'And you get told what goes on with the secret services?'

'Some of them, sure. Ben, our intel was a key part of their investigation. I sent them everything that you, me and Toru recorded inside that tunnel. They kind of owed me.'

Nodding, Ben said only, 'Your pal, Emma.'

Truby either didn't hear or chose to ignore that, saying, 'The people who rented the plane had US and UK passports. White, European, one male, one female, that's all they've released. Nothing to suggest any wrong doing. No criminal records.'

'Huh,' Ben said, chewing thoughtfully. 'So they're innocent?'

'They're both dead, so that's implied. Obviously it could still be a suicide mission.'

'I thought you said the plane's controls had been tampered with by remote?' Ben said. 'Doesn't that suggest that someone else was in on it? Whoever planted the remote control device on the plane.'

'Indeed,' agreed Truby. 'And that's where the trail goes cold.'

'They can't find the thing?'

'The device? They found it. But it's badly burned, beyond any useful recognition. It's going to take time to trace the component manufacturer. That's assuming whoever planted it didn't construct it themselves.'

'Crumbs. Poor Switzerland,' Ben said. 'Two horrible catastrophes within a week.'

'And you and me just happen to be around for both of them.'

This was starting to sound seriously ominous to Ben. 'You think that's going to be a problem?'

'Sure it is − it's gonna be a problem for whoever thought to get me involved,' Truby said, his voice dropping, the edge all steel.

'You'd have been on one of those buses, wouldn't you?'

Truby nodded. 'I would, at that.'

Now Ben hesitated. It couldn't possibly be that there was a connection − could it? Yet from Truby's heavy tone, he guessed that this was exactly what Truby was thinking. It made him wonder if this wasn't why Truby had kept his movements so quiet today.

Truby picked up his Coke and jiggled it slightly, agitating the four ice cubes that had floated to the surface. 'Ben, I think you and I ought to start planning an intervention.'

Ben caught his breath. 'What, with Gemini Force? Here?'

'Those two buses have vanished. The avalanche tracked right across the road they were on. You mark my words, they're buried. The fact that they haven't been found yet means that the vehicle's own GPS beacons are either non-functional or else they've been turned off. It's going to take a while to locate them. In the meantime, the folk aboard those coaches are going to start to find it awful cold. And claustrophobic. And after not much longer, they're going to start to run out of air.'

Agape, Ben asked, 'How much longer?'

Truby shrugged. 'Twenty people each bus, say a volume of fifteen metres by two and a half, throw in a factor for breathing a little more because of the cold, the average normal consumption of air over time . . .' He paused. 'You're talking a little under twenty-four hours.'

'Whoa,' Ben said. 'That's got to be enough though, right? I mean, it won't take all that long to dig them out once they've been found?'

'Maybe not,' Truby said, nodding. 'And yet. What can I tell you, Ben? There's something really off about all this. Terrorism in Switzerland? Who are they even targeting? It's not clear.'

'Bankers,' Ben said, thinking bitterly of the various crooked money-men with whom his own father had been forced to deal when financing the Sky High Hotel.

Casper Carrington had done his fair share of fraud, but he and his chief financial officer had taken the whole blame. None of the banking institutions he'd been working so hard to pay off had suffered at all. 'Everyone hates bankers, right?'

'I'm not a banker,' Truby pointed out. 'If not for a meeting I pulled out of my hat at the last minute, I'd have been on one of those coaches. And those people in the Jungfraujoch tunnel, they weren't all bankers.'

'So if not bankers, who?'

Truby shook his head, teeth worrying at his lower lip. 'I don't know. But I'd feel a whole lot safer with GF Two and our ice digger close by.'

— VIRAL —

'Hilja Juul, president of the European Central Bank. Werner Grieg, president of International Monetary Fund. Bob Talahassee, the Vice-President of the USA. Gennady Krupin, the head of the Russian investment bank, Mozno. Three more chiefs of top Swiss banks, as well as their partners. The heads of four more major banks based in London, Frankfurt and Brussels. And the CEOs of three global corporations that made the Forbes Top Ten last year. These are just some of the high-profile names involved in today's horrific avalanche in the Swiss town of Davos.'

The television news presenter sounded urgent, yet oddly excited. He was bundled up in a thick woollen coat and clutching a large microphone. He basked in bright camera lighting that glared like a beacon just outside the hotel's lobby, from where the report was being broadcast to billions of TV sets around the planet.

Ben watched Truby fold both arms across his chest as he pressed his chin down against the edge of his open shirt collar. 'They've released the names,' he said with an approving nod. 'Now watch the vultures descend. It's like Charles Tatum said – *Bad news sells best. Cause good news is no news.*'

'Who's Charles Tatum?'

'Oh, an old-time newspaper man,' Truby replied. He looked pensive. 'The kind with an instinct to keep an ace in the hole. A *movie* newspaper man,' he added, 'but he spoke for the lot of 'em.'

Inside Ben's pocket, his phone vibrated. Jasmine, again.

OMG ARE YOU WATCHING? It's just gone viral.

We're here! I'm looking at the guy who's doing the news, right now!

Sooooo. ;) I'm guessing a certain international rescue agency is going to be on its way to Davos? What with two of its most important members being on the ground – again. Or has JT decided to stay away? Not like THIS rescue could be kept secret.

Ben's lips twitched as he tried to stifle a smirk. As awful as the situation was, he could see why Jasmine was text-winking. It was exciting to be on the ground as a thing like this happened. Some of the most powerful, influential people in the world were in mortal danger. If Gemini Force did end up taking part in the rescue, it would be nigh on impossible to keep the agency secret. There would be massive media attention. Fame. Pictures of Ben in his uniform might appear on the news. Toru and James were probably more conventionally handsome, but being the youngest, Ben would probably get extra attention. For a moment, he wondered if that might be kind of cool.

But only for a *moment*. Then he started to see it from Truby's point of view. There might be issues with his ties to business. Envious competitors. Angry foreign governments, who hadn't been consulted – unlike the US government, apparently - and felt left out. There might be all sorts of grim side-effects.

Need to talk to JT now. Will look at phone on and off. x

KK. Hugs and stuff. Cuddly emoji that I don't know how to do.

Ben couldn't help smiling. Jasmine was just too cute.

A hotel official approached their table. 'Herr Truby, your syndicate room is ready.'

Truby stood. 'Let's go.'

Ben managed to wrap the remaining half of his croissant in a thick paper napkin before he took off after Truby and the be-suited, rather stiff hotel official. The man led them through to the conference centre section of the hotel, and used his security pass to open a door. It revealed a small room kitted out with a rectangular table on which had been placed two adjacent, iMac 27-inch screens, with a laptop attached and sitting between them. On a long side table against the wall were a coffee machine, a pale-blue glass bowl of multi-coloured coffee pellets and an array of glass tumblers, cups and saucers.

The hotel official bowed very slightly and said, in a soft German accent, 'Everything has been set up according to your specifications. If you should need anything else, Herr Truby, please call reception.'

'Everything looks great, Franz,' Truby said, his attention already on the computers. He turned briefly and snapped out a grin. 'We'll take it from here.'

After Franz had left, Ben watched Truby open up a Linux window into which he started typing lines of code. Pretty soon text was flashing back and forth across the screen, and windows were opening across all three screens. Within minutes the three screens were showing exactly the same display that he'd seen many times in the command centre of Gemini Force One. Some windows showed video footage, others showed a stream of rapidly flashing newsfeed information, with search terms highlighted and clustered around the subject. Ben immediately recognised the format of the information as the one that Denny Atalas, the chief of medicine's son on GF One, had set up for Truby. Denny's little piece of computer code had dazzled pretty much everyone on the base.

'How are you doing that? It looks just like it does back home.'

Truby winked. 'Remote access. Dietz put in a bunch of security layers to stop anyone hacking us. The last one is that he made me promise not to allow anyone from outside Gemini Force to overlook us.' Truby took a plastic bag containing a radio headset and earbuds from his pocket and slid it across the table to Ben. 'You might wanna listen in. But go ahead and guard the door, Ben.'

Ben moved back silently, placed his back to the door and then stuck his thumbs in his jeans pockets while he observed. The screens were showing footage from five different cameras, some of which, Ben guessed, were Davos town webcams, and others from newsfeeds. He could see the outside of security-surrounded Hotel le Dauphin, from where many snow-coated journalists were broadcasting their news reports, the top of the Weissfluh and the trail of avalanche disaster that led down one side of its slope. Other windows showed aerial footage of the search for the lost coaches. One was simply sweeping back and forth over an area that seemed to be mainly a mixture of dirty snow, ice and a smattering of powder from the snow that had been falling in the past hour – presumably from a helicopter.

Truby pointed to the window that showed this. 'The buses have got to be somewhere under all that. It's the only place where the fall is deep enough to cover the vehicles.'

'How deep?'

'Maybe ten metres above the coaches? Deep enough.'

'But they can dig through that OK. I mean,' Ben swallowed in a dry throat, hoping he wasn't wrong. 'It won't take twenty hours, will it?'

'I agree.'

'So are you not bothering with GF Two, then?'

Truby continued to stare at the screen. 'Might as well get 'em over. They're already in the air, with GF Nine.'

GF Nine was the ice-digger for which Truby had recently been purchasing some kind of upgraded controls. It was about the size of a hatchback car, a robotic machine that resembled a rolling conveyer belt, like the base of an army tank, with two arms attached at both ends, each holding out a rotating metallic bucket drum. The ice-digging machine, already being referred to as 'the Iceman' by James and Paul, was capable of robotic, rolling movement over rough terrain and even steep inclines. When it found a place to dig it somehow anchored itself and then the rotating drums got to work, melting the ice at the surface with a blast of microwaves to allow the drill a few precious seconds, during which they could get a good purchase on the material before the rotating drums began to systematically 'shave' layers away, rapidly descending into the hole they'd created, discarding ice dust in a fine spray behind the drums.

Ben hadn't seen 'the Iceman' in action, but he'd seen various computer animations of how it should work. He was looking forward to seeing the genuine article.

As he listened in to Truby discussing possible scenarios with Dietz and James, Ben allowed his mind to wander. To allow himself, for the first time, to wonder what it might be like inside those coaches. With no way of communicating with the outside world, and no idea how deeply they'd been buried. A collection of people that Ben guessed were used to getting their own way

– how would they handle it? Who would be brave, whose nerve would collapse as the fear began to bite?

The news coverage was already strangely unsympathetic to the missing conference delegates. In fact, everything Ben had heard so far had been breathless, more awestruck than compassionate. All across the globe, news agencies were reeling from the fact that this dreadful thing was happening to these particular people. No one seemed seriously worried that anything permanent would happen to them, and the race was definitely on to dig them out. But it did seem to be rapidly descending into an entertainment, a sideshow.

When Holden White appeared on the video stream from outside the hotel, Ben perked up. The rock star was dressed in a white mohair sweater and cream jeans, his signature colours when in public – white, cream and beige. His hair looked rumpled and his usually tidy, sparse beard slightly ragged. Almost as though he hadn't cleaned up after their adventure in the air.

'It's poetic justice, in't it? Like, how perfect do you need it to be? A bunch of wa – I mean – bankers and oligarchs, all cooped up, like sardines in a net. Forced to live in a tiny cramped space which I'm guessing has to be getting pretty rank. D'you know what I mean? Not like they're drinking champagne in there – least, not any more. No. They'll be bricking it. But d'you know what? Some of 'em, they probably deserve it. Some of 'em have taken decisions that have condemned millions of people all over the world to poverty.' White jabbed the air with the index finger of his left hand. 'I think sometimes the universe has a way of expressing its disgust. Cause if anyone needed a lesson it's this lot. Yeah, maybe a bit of fear is what they need. A bit of desperation. Maybe it'll make them realise that this is how most people in the world have to live, every day of their lives. Uncertain. Worrying if they'll be able to make ends meet. Scared.'

Truby was shaking his head by now, listening in obvious disbelief.

'Well,' Ben said after a moment. 'He's sort of got a point, hasn't he? It won't hurt them to get a sense of what so many people have to live with.'

At which point Truby swung around and faced him with an expression of bafflement. 'I expected better from you, Ben. The only reason I'm even listening to you right now is because you've personally put so much into helping those worse off than yourself. And because you know what it's like to feel trapped.'

'Yes, I do,' Ben replied quietly, calmly staring back at Truby with increasing resentment. 'And anyway, Holden is only saying what everyone's thinking.'

'Ben!' Truby said, exasperated. 'Listen to yourself! We could have been inside those coaches. You and me. For no other reason than we happen to be well-connected.'

'You are,' Ben said, sullenly. 'Not me; not anymore.'

Truby snorted. 'You think that people who think that way are going to see you as being any different to me?'

Ben didn't answer. But he remembered how White had told him, 'you're all right.'

Holden knew the difference. So what if the guy was using his fame to make a point? Maybe it was a point that needed to be made. It wasn't as though the bankers and the oligarchs were going to die. They were just going to suffer for a while. With any luck, this ordeal would help them to become better, more sympathetic, more considerate and merciful. If it did, wouldn't the world be better for that?

'Addison, James and Paul,' Truby told Ben, when he asked which Gemini Force crew were on their way to Davos. 'Rigel too – his sense of smell might just come in handy if they really can't find the coaches, but let's hope the local dogs can do that long before. And Toru, of course. He's flying 'em across.'

Ben cracked his knuckles, muttering, 'Excellent.' It was a downer to think of the conference delegates being buried any longer than was absolutely necessary. Yet he couldn't quite resist the tiniest hope that somehow, Gemini Force would be needed. When he mentioned this to Truby, however, he saw something akin to genuine worry darken the man's features. 'Not at all.'

'Yeah, fair enough, it could have been you in one of those coaches,' Ben said, trying to sound wise and understanding.

'That's not the reason,' Truby said, firmly. His expression grew even more wary. 'For once, I sincerely hope that Gemini Force isn't called upon.'

Truby didn't say any more and Ben didn't ask, because at that moment, his phone began to buzz. His phone was normally set on single buzz, but for Jasmine's messages it buzzed three times. Ben was already starting to associate the sensation of the phone's vibration in his jeans pocket with the pleasant anticipation of a text from Jasmine.

Dad says GF are getting in on the action. Rigel too! Are you going to help?

Ben replied,

Maybe! Although I get the feeling that JT would rather we sit this one out.

Huh. Probably something to do with the secrecy. The whole world is watching, after all.

Fair point!

Then Ben heard a dry voice at his shoulder. 'Benedict, if you could tear yourself away from your phone for a moment, maybe we can get ready to head out for some reconnaissance?'

Hurriedly, Ben stuffed his phone back into his jeans pocket. 'Reconnaissance?' he said, hopefully.

'I've hired a glider,' Truby said. 'Thought we'd go up to somewhere where we can overlook the zone that's been affected.'

'A glider? You know how to fly one of those?'

'First thing I learned to fly,' Truby said with an uncharacteristically reserved smile.

'Wouldn't a snowmobile be better? Or a chopper?'

'Snowmobile – probably. But the whole mountain will be closed off in the avalanche zone. And a heli – that's gonna attract a lot of attention. Very noisy. A glider – it's normal for those to just wind around in circles. We'll stay out of the way.' Truby reached down to unzip the black suitcase he'd just placed on the coffee table. He removed a large camera and handed it to Ben, who began to examine it. 'That's a Nikon D4S digital SLR. I want you to shoot as much as you can. We're gonna find us a gnarly vantage point; scope us out a little of the rescue scene.'

Ben glanced up. 'Gnarly?'

Truby grinned. 'No reason we can't enjoy this, kiddo.'

They reached the airfield almost an hour later, hampered on the way by slow-moving snow ploughs that were still carving their way through the most recent snowfall. In places, the snow they heaped at the side of the roads would reach as high as Ben's shoulder; a grit-filled wall of icy snow.

At the airfield it was the same story; the single, short runway was being cleared by ploughs and a Kiitokori de-icing vehicle. When eventually they did manage to get into the air, Ben glanced at his phone to see that he'd missed a bunch of texts from Jasmine. The first one began with the tantalising phrase,

I'm going to have The Talk with Jonah.

'Use that goddamn phone for something useful,' Truby interrupted. 'Call Dietz and put him on speaker. I want a sitrep re. *Leo* and the crew, and then I need to know the latest on the rescue scene.'

Reddening at the implied telling-off, Ben did as Truby had asked. Within a minute, Dietz was talking them through the news about the local mountain rescue effort. 'They seem to have decided on a location. It's more or less directly underneath a place where the mountain has a steep overhang. Odd, because according to the maps of the region, that whole slope is covered with avalanche snow bridges.'

'Maybe we'll look into that,' Truby murmured.

Listening, Ben took a closer look at the controls of the digital single lens reflex Nikon camera. Carefully, he attached the 400mm telephoto lens and set the camera to automatic focus and continuous shooting mode. Then he tested the weight of the apparatus, gauging how much support he'd need to give to the long lens. When Truby asked if he was all set, Ben said, 'Aye aye, cap'n.'

He didn't mention it to Truby, but this was actually Ben's first time in a glider, and he was surprisingly nervous. His father, Casper, had had a phobia of flight in any kind of small aircraft. Carrington International hadn't even had a private jet, unlike a few corporations of similar size. The official story had been that Casper Carrington didn't like to miss an opportunity to learn from another company's hospitality – it all went into making him a better hotelier. The reality, however, was that he had a terror of flying in anything smaller than a Boeing 737. That fear had been transmitted into an order when it came to his own family, but Caroline hadn't always enforced it – not when it came to heli-skiing. Gliders, however, had been strictly forbidden. Ben had turned down at least three invitations from school friends whose older siblings had qualified in the sport.

Now that they were off the ground and descending in large, lazy circles over the snow-blanketed landscape beyond the buildings of Davos, Ben felt a creeping sense of unease. The silence was downright eerie. No sound but the slight burr of the super-light alloy wings of their craft slicing through the air. Ben stared hard at the digital image on the camera's screen, trying to distance himself from the reality of being in the air in a flimsy cockpit, held aloft only by the physical forces of thermal uplift and two broad wings. If anything happened, if anything went wrong, the only exit strategy was a kind of controlled fall. He risked a cautious glance at Truby in the pilot's seat, both hands on the controls. There was an almost beatific smile on his lips.

Well at least he's happy, Ben thought.

'OK, Ben, we're approaching the mountain slope, on the left. I want photos of the whole area. Video first, then give me a tight focus, like, ten metres per shot, and just keep it on burst mode until we've got everything.'

Ben obeyed, silently gulping down his nervousness

every time the glider lurched at a segment of cooler air, or banked into a turn. *It's all under control, it's all under control.* He barely managed to concentrate on what he was photographing, all his attention required to follow Truby's instructions.

Beneath the slope, he could see the red-painted helicopter and vehicles of the mountain rescue. Red ski suits were dotted around one spot. Ben could see at least three dogs with the rescue crew. Every so often, the sound of their barking even reached as high as the glider, which continued to flow like silk through the clear blue sky.

'I think they may have found the coaches,' Ben said. His finger pressed on the camera shutter as he continued to shoot.

'That's good news for everyone,' Truby said. 'Everyone except the news agencies,' he added, thoughtfully.

A sudden rumble on the mountain went directly to Ben's bones – a low boom, muffled and long, followed by a high-pitched cracking – the sound of ice breaking. The sound ripped through the clean peacefulness at their altitude, jolting Truby hard enough that his grip faltered for just a second. Ben felt the Nikon camera sliding through his fingers for a moment. His entire body jerked forward, lunging for the expensive equipment before it hit the floor of the glider. From the pilot's seat he heard a rapid intake of breath as the nose of the glider dipped.

Then they were pitched forward, diving fast. The fir-tree-dotted slope of the mountain rushed at the glider's tiny, bubble-like windscreen. Ben would have screamed if he'd had the air for it. But he had nothing in his chest except a solid lump of pure, wild fear.

━ BROKEN MOUNTAIN ━

As the glider barrelled towards the mountain, Ben clutched the camera in his right hand and curled the fingers of his left around the nearest hard surface – a metal runner beneath his seat. He screwed his eyes tightly shut. The last thing he saw was Truby leaning forward, teeth bared in a rictus grin, one fist grasping the rudder control and pulling, hard.

The glider banked to the right. Ben peeked then, watching the tip of the wing as it rose, until it seemed almost vertical and he was leaning, almost horizontal. He dared a quick glance through the right-hand window, stared down, vertically, past the milky-silver expanse of the glider's wing, to the trees and snow below.

A cloud of powder was rising from the mountain, heading straight down the slope. For an instant, the view through the cockpit was a thing of terrible beauty; nature in its most powerful majesty – a river of snow and ice hurtling through fir trees, felling them in its wake.

'Come on, come on!' muttered Truby. The glider continued its left-hand turn, until they'd cleared the slope and the aircraft's nose was pointing into clear air. As they straightened up, both Ben and Truby released long, heated breaths. Hardly another second had passed before Truby was once again insisting, 'Did you get the shot?'

Ben lifted the telephoto lens to the window, twisted around to face through the rear of the glider, and began to take more pictures. There wasn't really time to focus, but as he allowed his fingers to work automatically, and swept the camera around the entire field of vision, he looked past the camera's screen and began to take in what he saw.

It was more dreadful than he'd dared imagine. The powder cloud had moved so fast, it had taken less than a minute to reach the heap of frozen debris already stacked around the skirt of the mountain. Where the mountain rescue team had been before, now there was only pale grey mist, like morning fog settling over a marsh.

'Oh no,' Ben whispered. He began to rake his gaze over the nearby slope, and along. Maybe he was mistaken? Maybe he'd somehow got all turned around in the air and was looking in the wrong place. Eventually, his eyes landed on Truby, who continued to stare directly ahead. His face looked drawn, tense with latent rage.

'The rescue crew,' Ben began, choking on the words. 'They're . . . They . . .'

'They're buried,' finished Truby, biting off the words. The glider was completing a circle now, returning to their original position but at a safe distance from the mountain. 'The slope, Ben. Look at the slope, will you? Get the photos.'

That's when Ben finally saw what he'd failed to

notice before, all the pieces of the larger picture coming together, the dozens of moments in time that he'd captured with the camera, each one just a tiny part of the whole story. Now he faced the mountain, his back hard and straight against his seat, and he saw it; the broken mountain.

Poking out and in dark contrast against the white of the snow, in at least four places, were the twisted and shattered remains of avalanche snow bridges.

'The snow bridges,' Ben said, gasping. 'They look they've been . . .' He turned to look at Truby. 'They've been destroyed. That sound we heard, just before the avalanche started up again. It was . . . it must have been explosives.'

'Several, I should think,' agreed Truby.

Ben raised the camera once again. This time he was careful, methodical, training the lens on each image of blackened, smoking metal that stuck out like knives from beneath the snow. Underneath each broken bridge was a trail of devastation – the path of the avalanche.

As he took the photos, Ben wondered what kind of maniac would do something like this – deliberately cause an avalanche. No one would have been on the ski slopes by now, not after the last avalanche had shut down the entire mountain. Only the rescuers.

Then it struck him. Someone didn't want the rescuers to do their job. They were willing to kill, or at least risk the lives of the rescue workers, in order to stop the people in those coaches being rescued.

The glider turned again, this time towards the left. With icy calm now, Ben stared straight down through the window of the cockpit as the craft banked, at the ground below, now coated with the final settlings of the avalanche, a fine, dirty-white powder.

'The first avalanche was no accident,' he said, dully. Truby didn't reply for a few moments, but Ben nodded to himself. It was the only thing that made sense of this second avalanche. The snow bridges had been sabotaged. Someone had known that the coaches would be going past this route. They'd engineered the first avalanche, as well as its follow-up.

Fifteen minutes under a snow heap could kill you. The rescue workers might live – some of them might manage to crawl out, others might be reached by a secondary crew – assuming there were any rescue workers left to help them.

But the people inside the buried coaches were now at least a few more hours away from being rescued. The job was beginning to look a lot less possible.

'It's a good thing you sent for Gemini Force,' mumbled Ben. He tried to resist the impulse to twist in his seat and take a final look behind the glider at the heap of fresh snow that now blanketed the entire rescue area. But he couldn't, not completely. As the glider floated towards the airfield beyond Davos, Ben's gaze became fixated on the spot, his imagination barely able to venture any closer to those buried rescue workers.

Buried alive, trapped, freezing cold and alone. It had

to be one of the most horrible ways to die. Slow enough to be terrifying, even if it wasn't too painful.

'How long until *Leo* and the others get here?'

'Two hours.'

'Too late for the rescue workers,' Ben said, too quickly to realise that the comment might not be welcome. Truby didn't respond.

'Who would do this?' Ben said, thinking aloud.

'I've been wondering about that since that plane crashed into the Jungfraujoch tunnel.'

Staring, Ben asked, 'You're so sure there's a connection?'

'More than ever.'

In his inside jacket pocket, Ben's phone buzzed three times.

Are you watching what your big hero Holden White is saying?

Jasmine's text was followed by a link to an online video. When Ben clicked on it, he saw Holden White being filmed standing in the lobby of Hotel le Dauphin. He stood tall in white skinny jeans and a white mohair pullover that reached halfway down his thighs, gesticulating with his right index finger.

'All I'm saying is that maybe it's *meant to be*, yeah? Someone up there obviously doesn't want those bankers and those flippin' *oligarchs* to have a nice day. D'you know what I mean? If you look for meaning in the universe, sometimes the universe finds a way to give an answer,' White was saying.

'Gee,' Truby muttered, sarcastically. 'Bleached hair, bleached teeth; guess he bleached his brains for the matching set.'

Ben didn't know how to respond. As one of the most glamorous people on the scene, the young rock star was bound to be interviewed by the media. He was bound to want to make his usual points about injustice. Normally, Ben would have totally supported him, and risen to his defence against comments like Truby's. But he knew what White didn't yet know, what the world was yet to discover.

The avalanche wasn't just the universe's way of correcting some unfairness. It was not some accidentally righteous backlash against those who accumulated too much power. This was a malignant, deliberate attempt to kill people – innocent working people just as much as the rich and powerful with their 'hangers-on'.

Holden White certainly knew how to grab a headline. But for the first time, Ben began to wonder whether his judgement was all it could be.

'He doesn't know,' Ben said after a while, feebly. 'You can't think that Holden would say something so mind-bogglingly *naff*, not if he knew. Can you?'

'What I think,' Truby said, seeming to choose his words carefully, 'is that I may have underestimated young Mister White. *Severely* underestimated.'

━ WINGNUT ━

'All right, Ben mate! Over 'ere!'

Holden White was already in the lobby when Ben and Truby returned to Hotel le Dauphin at ten-fifteen in the morning. Still wearing his ski outfit, he must have been watching the revolving doors at the entrance to the lobby's marble atrium, because the moment that Ben and Truby walked through, White began to push his way through his entourage, towards them. Ben could sense Truby's impatience when the rock singer planted himself in their path, effectively obstructing any further progress.

'Good thing you changed your mind about that VIP trip, innit?' White said, addressing Truby.

Beside him, Ben saw Truby visibly stiffen. 'Apparently so,' he said, quietly.

'I'm getting a sort of vibe off you, Jason Truby. Reckon you're a bit narked — am I right?' White said this last sentence with a note of sadness. 'Cheer up, mate, it never 'appened. Not to you, at least.'

'I imagine you think I should be right there with the rest of those guys,' Truby said, laconically. He crossed his arms. 'Isn't that right? After all, I am the CEO of Trubycom. Tell me this, White, why not you, too?

You're CEO of Holden White Enterprises, are you not?'

'I got nothing like that,' White said, emphatic. 'I don't care about money, me, I never have. It's all about the music.'

Truby broke into astonished laughter, yet White's expression, entirely sincere, didn't shift. Ben felt his chest swelling with pride on behalf of his favourite rock singer.

'I'm glad you didn't go,' White said, his eyes still on Truby's while he gestured with a nod at Ben. 'Cause this one 'ere wouldn't have been too happy if you were one of them that's trapped. Right, Ben, mate?'

Ben found himself nodding. 'Of course.'

'Ben's all right,' White said, for the second time since they'd met. 'Ben is *sound*. A credit to his mam, from what I've heard. And to whoever's been keeping an eye out for him since she died. Even if he is the son of a rich bastard who'd be in prison by now, if he wasn't dead.'

In the shocked silence that followed, Ben could only find himself agreeing. Casper Carrington had indeed turned out to be a less than ideal role model. In his own mind, this was why Ben consciously followed his mother's example wherever possible, and avoided his father's.

'I got a feeling that Jason Truby is partly to thank for your *exemplary* behaviour, Ben Carrington,' continued White. 'So d'you know what? *I'm* glad he's not in one of them coaches, an' all.'

'That would weigh heavily on your conscience, would it?' Truby said, smoothly sarcastic.

White tweaked an eyebrow. 'Who, me? It's nowt to do with me, mate.'

Ben spoke up for the first time. 'Holden, you've kind of got to admit though, with the way you've been talking, it does sort of sound as though you sympathise with whoever did this.'

Holden's smirk held steady, but with obvious effort. Through a smile he said, '*Whoever* did this? Ooer, sounds ominous. I thought we were talking about, like, an "act of God".'

Truby placed a hand on the middle of Ben's back and began to steer him past White. 'You'll have to excuse us, Mr White.' As they moved past White, Truby leaned closer to Ben and whispered a single word. '*Quiet.*'

But to Ben's surprise, White wasn't so easily deterred from his mission. In another moment he'd danced around the pair and reached the elevator before them.

'Hang about, you two. What exactly are you saying?'

Ben was itching to speak up, and tightened his fists in an effort to restrain himself, but he couldn't help casting an imploring look at Truby.

Just tell him that the snow bridges have been blown up! Or else he's going to keep saying things that make him sound like a dangerous idiot, Ben thought.

To his mild astonishment, however, Truby simply gave the singer a benign smile and then stepped around him and into the elevator as the doors opened. 'Take it easy, pal,' he said, casually.

As the lift doors closed off Ben and Truby from everything else, Ben said, 'Whoa. Awkward.'

'Holden White is acting like a wingnut,' Truby replied, quiet but emphatic. 'Hardly surprising. The kid is nineteen and he's already on top of the world. Either that – or else he's something a lot more dangerous.'

'What did you mean when you said you'd underestimated him? You don't seriously think Holden White's got anything to do with this?'

'That *would* appear to be beyond a guy of White's somewhat youthful judgement,' Truby said, sounding as though he and Ben were in agreement. Which annoyed Ben, he realised. He'd never openly suggested that White was anything but clever. It was just that a guy like White, someone who felt that passionately about social injustice and inequality, and was a famous singer too, could easily let his mouth run away with him. He wouldn't be the first rock star to get into trouble for an off-the-cuff quip.

'Holden White is not daft,' Ben said, stubbornly. 'He's just pointing out something that is screamingly obvious to everyone watching what's going on out there. Why shouldn't he be the one to say it?'

The lift doors slid open, but Truby didn't move. Instead, he watched Ben with something that looked like amazement. 'Are you serious?'

There was something faintly intimidating about

Truby's attitude. It felt a lot like fatherly disapproval. For the first time he could remember, Ben felt a flash of anger towards Truby's presumption. Truby wasn't his dad. His dad was dead. And as White had pointed out, Ben's dad had been exactly the kind of person that had showed the world that rich people were not to be trusted.

Ben stuck his arm across the lift door, holding it open. He faced Truby with open defiance. 'You can't *actually* be accusing a guy like Holden White of being responsible for planting those bombs. He's a musician!'

'And a pretty idiotic one, from what I've seen,' Truby said, nodding. 'But you never can tell.'

An incredulous gasp escaped Ben's lips. 'He isn't idiotic. Have you ever listened to his lyrics?'

'I have not, Benedict, I'd never heard of the guy until you and I met. I'm judging purely on the basis of what I've seen while we've been in Davos.'

'Well,' Ben said, 'if you *had* you'd know. Holden is smart. But, remember, I've actually *met* the kind of person who does a thing like this - Minos Winter, the guy who blew up Horizon Alpha. And Jason, I can tell you this, there's a world of difference. Holden White is a *poet*.' As Ben's speech grew more impassioned, he felt his resentment for Truby's narrow-minded suspicion growing. 'He's a social commentator – he speaks out against poverty and injustice.'

'Oh sure, the guy is a living saint,' Truby said,

sneering. 'I mean, it's not like anyone pays him for his books or his TV appearances or his concerts.'

Ben withdrew his arm, feeling an icy breeze sweep through him. Truby was being so . . . so *smug*. It really didn't suit him.

'I'm going back to the lobby,' Ben said, coldly.

'That wouldn't be wise,' Truby said, stepping out of the lift. 'Come on, Ben, let's go talk to GF Two.'

Ben shook his head. 'I don't fancy it. Not just now.'

'Oh I see – you want to head back down and talk to the dingbat, instead?'

For a second or two, Truby's eyes blazed at Ben's easy defiance. They faced each other and Ben could see Truby making a calculation. Would he feel it was necessary to give him a direct order? Ben felt his pulse fluttering as he waited for Truby's response. And found that he was actually surprised when the man withdrew his hand from where it had taken over in holding the lift doors open.

'Go ahead, Ben,' Truby said, his voice deadly calm. 'Go learn something.'

━ #NEWGAME ━

Down in the lobby, Ben walked straight past Holden White and his adoring entourage, and headed back into the streets of Davos. He was still seething about the apparently abrupt shift in Truby's attitude towards him. *Go learn something*, Truby had instructed, in a tone that was balanced perfectly between disdain and dismissal.

Ben was *always* learning. All he did was learn – learn how to be good enough, strong enough, brave enough and knowledgeable enough to be a fully-fledged member of Gemini Force. It didn't mean that he worshipped the ground on which Jason Truby walked. Now that there was someone else that Ben looked up to, Truby seemed annoyed. You might even say he was threatened. To imply – even via the darkest humour – that someone like Holden White would ever get involved in a vile act of terrorism – it was just unthinkable. It was as though Truby were telling Ben – *you can't have any role models that I haven't approved.*

'*And* he's not even my dad,' Ben muttered resentfully, loud enough that an elderly woman walking her dog on the pavement, just ahead of him, turned around in surprise. Ben ignored her, pushed his chin down into the collar of his jacket. He tried to jam his hands into his pockets, but his fingers bumped against the hotel freebies he'd stuffed inside. He pulled a pair of leather gloves from an inside jacket pocket and put them on instead.

The sky thickened with whiteness as flakes began to fall. Pedestrians glanced upwards, some annoyed, some fearful. They pulled hoods over their heads and tied their scarves a little tighter. Ben turned a corner into a pedestrianised shopping street. He stopped under a gold-and-white striped awning in front of a bakery, gazing inside at the display of marzipan fruits, Linzertortes and decorated gingerbreads. He removed a glove, plucked his phone from his jeans pocket and called Jasmine.

'Hi,' he said the instant she answered, warm and breathless. She wasn't in class. Fantastic.

'Hello!' She sounded surprised. 'What's up?'

'Oh, I've just had a bit of a falling out with Truby.'

'What? Really?'

Ben tried to laugh. 'He's got this insane theory that Holden White is somehow behind the avalanche thing that's trapped the VIPs in those coaches. Obviously, I pointed out how bonkers that is. Which he didn't like to hear. As you can imagine.'

'Gosh, yes, I can. Wow. That's actually pretty crazy. He's not much older than you.'

'I know – right?' agreed Ben. He was surprised at just how relieved he was to hear someone else give the sensible response to Truby's notion. 'It's insane. Even if you were some kind of wingnut – as Truby puts it

– trying to make a point about the evils of capitalism, the super-rich and all – the *rescuers* who just got blitzed, they're completely innocent.'

'They are,' Jasmine said, sadly. 'Are you watching TV? A new crew is on their way now. To dig out the rescuers first, I guess. And then they'll have to get back to digging out the coaches. If there's still time.'

'I'm in the street,' Ben told her. 'I'm looking at a patisserie.'

'Oh. I really wish I would be with you.'

'We could rent a helicopter and a couple of shovels and go out there and help. To be honest, that's exactly what I feel like doing right now,' Ben said, glumly.

'You're good enough to fly a helicopter alone now?'

'Yeah, I could manage. It won't be long until I get my licence.'

'Oh Ben, I wish. Instead, I have to be stuck in school.' She sounded so sweet and familiar. Ben was a little astonished by how much hearing Jasmine's voice made him want to reach for her and pull her into his arms.

On the other end of the phone there was a sudden and sharp intake of breath. 'Ben – you need to get to a TV right now!'

'What's going on?'

'I have to go, my teacher's calling us out of the common room . . . go find a television, Ben! Bye, I love you.'

Ben's ears were ringing as he realised what Jasmine had just said.

I love you. Did it count if you said it like that? The ending to a phone conversation, an urgent one at that; one that had ended without warning, totally abrupt? Her words had him so thoroughly bemused, that when he touched his chilled fingers to his cheeks he was astonished to find the skin was hot. He warmed his fingers there for a few seconds, cursing the fact that he'd left his proper winter gloves in the car that Truby had rented to take them out to the airfield. His leather gloves were sensitive, allowing for nimble finger movement, but they didn't entirely shut out the biting ice of the wind.

Jasmine had probably just blurted it out, an automatic response, kind of 'love ya, bye!' type of thing. Still – was he meant to ignore it? Or what? If she had been serious, surely he'd be in trouble if he ignored her words?

Then he remembered what Jasmine had said just before the 'I love you'.

Go find a television.

Ben was in the process of tugging at the leather fingers of his gloves when he felt a nudge in his ribs. He turned, startled at the sight of Holden White, now bundled up in a sleek coat of cream-coloured faux-fur. White's hands were deep in pockets that hung level with his hips, one elbow digging into Ben's side before the singer dodged, playfully. A teasing grin was on his lips as White said, 'Stare at them pies any longer and you'll turn into one.'

Ben chuckled, genuinely amused. 'Would you like to try one? The Linzertorte's really good.'

'No man, too sweet; I prefer a nice sausage roll, me.'

They looked at each other for a second or two, Ben trying to work out what Holden White was doing in the street. Could it be . . . was it possible that White had followed him? Realistically, Ben couldn't work out how else he'd have ended up at the bakery so soon after Ben had seen him in the hotel lobby – not unless he was on the hunt for baked goods.

'I'm not sure they've got sausage rolls exactly,' Ben said. 'But they'll have some kind of savoury pastry.' He made as if to stand aside. 'Were you going in?'

But White didn't move, apart from rocking back and forth slightly on the heels of the blue suede mountain boots at the end of his white skinny jeans. Ben had to make an effort not to stare. This was getting odd now. It was as if White were trying to think something up on the spot. As if he was nervous.

Why does he care what I think about him?

'We could get a coffee,' White suggested. 'And one of them buns.'

Ben hesitated. 'I'd like to,' he said, with absolute honesty. 'But a friend just told me that there's something I need to see on TV.'

White simpered, 'Your girlfriend, was it?'

'Who?'

'What you was on the phone to just now?'

'Oh.' Ben blinked. How long had White been watching him? 'Sort of, yes.'

White turned around, now facing the other way

down the street. Briskly he said, 'Shall we be off, then?'

'Where?'

'To find a telly? The main shopping street is down there. Reckon at least one shop is bound to sell electronics and that.'

Ben turned to go after White, but slowly. White *had* followed him out of the hotel. It was the only explanation that made sense. Why? Was it that White was trying in some way to get to Jason Truby, via Ben?

He sped up, catching up with White who was waving both arms and then pointing into a building. Yes, it might be that. Maybe White was one of those celebrities who wanted everyone to like them, and got all hot and bothered when someone was indifferent. It was kind of pathetic, Ben realised, but fame did weird things to people. He really hoped that wasn't White's problem.

He arrived at the window into which Holden White was frantically pointing. It wasn't an electronics shop, but a boutique hotel with a HDTV display in the reception area. It was displaying the news. What Ben saw next on the screen made him totter towards the glass door, reaching out with both hands just in time to stop himself falling onto the panel.

'It's a flippin' spaceship!' White was dancing about like a crazed loon, gesticulating and laughing. He jabbed a single finger at the screen. 'Top one! It must be one of Richard Branson's new planes. The ones going to space. What's it doing in Switzerland?'

Ben ignored the babble that continued to flow from

Holden White's mouth, transfixed by the sight – on *television news* – of GF Two landing in the airfield near Davos. In amazement, he read the ticker-tape writing that streamed below the images.

UNKNOWN AGENCY ARRIVES TO ASSIST RESCUE OF TRAPPED VIPS IN DAVOS AVALANCHE. SWISS GOVERNMENT CLEARS MYSTERY RESCUE AGENCY TO DIG FOR BURIED RESCUERS. SEARCH CONTINUES FOR TWO COACHLOADS OF DELEGATES TO THE WORLD ECONOMIC FORUM.

The television screen was showing a group of eleven people clad in ski outfits of various colours and styles. They appeared to be protesting, carrying placards with the slogans:

THE GAME OF CAPITALISM IS RIGGED. END THE GAME. #NEWGAME

The camera angle widened and Ben saw that the protestors were making a circle. What was going on? He took out his phone, selected the radio app and clicked on BBC World Service. He began to listen, staring through the glass at the screen inside the hotel's tiny lobby.

'Davos, Switzerland, where thirty-eight VIP delegates from the World Economic Forum are trapped in two coaches, buried beneath tonnes of snow and ice, as well as eight rescue workers who were buried by a second avalanche less than twenty minutes ago. In a shocking development, a *second* rescue party appears to have been prevented from reaching the original rescuers. We're getting reports that a *circle of protestors* has descended on the rescue site, recently covered by a second fall of avalanche debris, and is blocking access to all rescuers.'

Holden White turned to Ben with a regretful nod. 'See? This is punishment, man. It's retribution. A human shield, yeah! The universe is balancing things out.'

Ben's phone was already buzzing as he lifted it to dial Truby's number. He was too stunned to be able to form a reply to White's comment. A text from Truby – three words.

He looked at White. 'I have to go back to the hotel.'

White allowed his attention to shift from the screen, on which GF Two was landing and being surrounded by a fleet of Swiss military vehicles. 'Give you a lift, if you want,' he offered. 'My driver's just parked round the corner.'

Before Ben could reply, a white VW Passat was pulling out of the traffic onto the main road that ran across the pedestrianised zone. It swerved into the shopping street, scattering people in its path.

The car was heading directly for Ben and White.

White threw one arm around Ben, his full weight against the boy's shoulder as he shoved Ben aside. Before both toppled against the brick wall of the hotel, Ben heard White say, 'Bloody paparazzi!'

Brakes screeched and snow chains rattled noisily as the tyres skated over hard-packed snow. The car skidded to a standstill less than half a metre from Ben's outstretched hand, trapping the two of them against the wall. The rear passenger door opened. With a jolt of unease, Ben noticed the black tint of the windows. Beside him, he felt the muscles of White's arm tensing up, no doubt preparing for some snap-happy photographer to emerge and shove a lens in his face. But the door remained ajar, and inside the car – who could say? The windows made it impossible to see anything of its occupants.

Then White was shoving Ben aside, one hand still

clutching his arm as he pushed past, yanking on the door and shouting insults at the driver.

Something clicked into place; months of training from James Winch triggered Ben's now heightened awareness of physical danger. He wrenched his arm from Holden White's grip just in time to see a figure emerging from the car door. He'd pivoted and was already sprinting away when he was rugby tackled to the ground from behind. He threw up both hands just in time to prevent his face smashing into the icy snow that was heaped at the edge of the pavement.

The man who'd attacked him was snaking his way up Ben's back, trying to get enough weight over his centre to pin Ben down. Wriggling, Ben flipped himself around so that he was facing his attacker. The man was clad in black from head to toe, including a knitted beanie pulled low, over coldly staring, blue eyes. He caught a glimpse of a sadistic grin just before a fist flew towards his face. But Ben's hands – both still free – were already snapping into position to protect him from the blow, which he'd fully expected. While the attacker tried to get a second punch in, Ben's hips bucked, throwing the attacker forwards, his punch landing in the crusty lump of snow just beyond.

Ben sensed immediate tension in his assailant's muscles.

James had warned him of this – many times.

'There'll come a moment when the guy attacking you will realise that you know how to fight. If he's a trained fighter he'll know that to underestimate you could be fatal. And he won't know, in that instant, how strong you are. It might be the single moment of weakness.'

Ben didn't waste any time. He grabbed the man's left arm and pulled it flush to his own body, simultaneously grape-vining his right leg around the attacker's left. With a surge of triumphant energy, Ben pushed his hips upwards again, felt the man's weight dislodge as he began to roll to the ground. Then Ben was on top, staring victoriously into the bewildered eyes of his attacker.

He heard the screech of the Passat's snow chains as the car slid up the road, slamming to a halt just behind and to his left. He heard car doors bursting open.

Ben's victory lasted less than three seconds. The next thing he felt was the hard edge of a gun's muzzle being crammed tightly into his left ear.

'Don't turn. Get up, slowly.'

When he hesitated, he heard the unmistakeable click of the pistol's safety being removed. 'Up,' repeated the voice to his left. Stumbling slightly, Ben rose. The moment that he'd opened up a space between them, the attacker's knee thudded into Ben's groin. A burst of white hot pain shot through him. He felt his insides lurch in panic.

'Yeah – you deserved that,' snickered the man with the gun.

Ben flinched, as if from a stinging slap. *He knew that voice.* The unseen man to his left opened the door. 'Inside.'

Ben staggered against the side of the car. His legs felt like jelly. He wanted to be sick. The pain was subsiding now, but the shock still hadn't. Dimly, he looked around, searching for Holden White. He was nowhere to be seen. The hesitation seemed to enrage the man with the gun, who ground the muzzle of the pistol even harder against the side of Ben's head.

'Inside!'

In despair now, Ben glanced around, backing towards the open door of the VW Passat. There was no sign of Holden White, but there had to be some other witness to this, someone who'd help? Finally, he dared to look at the man with the gun. He too was dressed in black, wore a beanie, but also, copper-tinted Aviator sunglasses. His eyes were dark and his chin covered with a scrub of beard.

The first attacker was on his feet now, heading menacingly towards Ben. A snow-encrusted boot was thrust into his face. Reflexes forced his eyelids closed as the boot's rubber sole ground against his mouth. He tasted salt and grit. The boot pounded into his jaw, pushing him further back into the car. The pressure split his lower lip, spilling blood across his chin. He reached for the inside door handle but when it flapped uselessly, Ben realised that the child lock system was engaged. The driver and front passenger doors slammed shut as the two men who'd attacked him resumed their positions.

The car jerked into gear. Ben was thrown backwards. When finally, a moment later, he managed to sit up, he found himself face to face with the barrel of a SIG–Sauer automatic pistol. It was in the hands of the first attacker. Beneath the opaque gaze of copper-tinted sunglasses, in the front mirror, Ben could see that the driver was smiling.

'Well hello, Benedict Carrington.'

Fear spiked through him at the sound of his own name.

He knew that voice. A British accent, northern, although nothing like the broad, rapid-fire delivery of Holden White. With a beard of several days' growth, the man looked quite different to the last time that Ben had seen him. Yet, just hearing those four words unlocked a memory that contained more dread than Ben could believe was possible.

Unleashed, those feelings began to flood his nervous system until he could scarcely breathe.

'Oh.' Reflected, a menacing grin spread across the driver's features. 'I see you remember me. Good to know I made such an impression.'

When Ben came back to himself, he realised that he was pressed deep into the seat, as far away as he could get from the owner of that voice and that dangerous smile.

Minos Winter.

'What . . . what are you doing here?'

'Working, Ben. What about you? Are *you* working? I see that *Gemini Force* are in town.'

Ben's thoughts raced, trying to piece together what he

could say and what he couldn't. The mercenary – Minos Winter – knew Ben's face, just as Ben knew his. The last time they'd seen each other, Winter had taken Ben prisoner on the platform supply vessel he'd used to make his getaway from the deepwater oil drilling platform, Horizon Alpha. Winter had been preparing to torture Ben in order to force Addison to give up information about Gemini Force. Thanks to a timely intervention by Rigel, and help from their Brazilian crew-mate, Julia Bencke, they'd escaped. But as Ben stared with glazed eyes at his captor, he realised that the fear of Winter's threats had never quite left him. Random thoughts flew through his mind, refusing to become organised.

Minos Winter. Terrorism. Holden White.

Could they be connected? Ben's mind stalled, as if unable or unwilling to develop the theory any further.

He was vaguely aware of the VW Passat making a U-turn, a right turn and then disappearing into a wall. As darkness enveloped the car, Ben grasped that they'd driven into an underground car park, an automatically operated door sliding into place behind them. The next thing he was aware of was the glare of a white light shining directly into his face. Minos Winter disappeared into its halo. Ben raised one hand to shield his eyes.

'Jason Truby?' he heard Winter say. 'We've got Benedict Carrington.'

⟿ OLD TIMES ⟾

'Isn't this just like old times, hey Carrington?'

From behind a gag of metallic insulation tape, Ben glared up at the grinning face of Minos Winter. Blood seeped from his torn lip and into his mouth. Every couple of minutes Ben was forced to swallow a mouthful of blood and saliva. His limbs were bound to the arms and legs of a wooden chair, snapped into place with plastic handcuffs. Towering over Ben, Winter's scrub of beard made him look older than when they'd met on *PSV-Macondo*; maybe as old as forty.

'I suppose you're wondering how I know your name . . . Ben.' Winter was silent for a few seconds, his smile falling away as his expression grew vague, introspective. When he spoke again, he leaned over Ben, close enough that Ben could smell stale cigarettes and coffee on his breath.

'You've a very recognisable face, Ben Carrington. When I saw you on the *PSV-Macondo*, d'you know what I thought? I actually wondered if you might be one of those teenage YouTubers or something, like your new best friend, Holden White. I knew I'd seen you on YouTube. Don't even want to tell you how many of those videos I watched, trying to find you.'

Ben's heart was racing hard enough that his breathing had turned into a noisy rasping through his nose, fluttering across a crinkle in the duct tape that covered his mouth. He could feel a thread of blood on his chin. It was true, there had to be dozens of homemade videos of the rescue of the two pilots that he and his mother had mounted at the opening of the Carrington Sky High Hotel in Abu Dhabi.

Winter reached forward, bent slightly and picked at the edge of the duct tape, peeling it carefully from Ben's face.

'Now it's time for *you* to talk, Ben. That gold mine in South Africa, where all the illegal miners were trapped - that was Gemini Force, wasn't it? And the ANPECO refinery in the Dominican Republic – the one where a mysterious fireman was seen flying around in a jet-pack – that was Gemini Force, too.'

It wasn't easy, but Ben managed not to react. Winter watched his eyes for a few seconds, then chuckled, very softly. 'I was hoping you'd confirm some of this. The profiling software says that there's a ninety-five per cent probability that it was Gemini Force. And *you* - you're the one that connects everything to Truby.'

He paused, stood for a moment, walked over to the other side of the chair to which Ben was tied. Then once again, Winter crouched at the knees until his face was level with Ben's. 'How did it happen, Ben? Did Truby fall for your mother? You couldn't blame him for that – I've seen photos of the countess. Her gorgeous, him one of the super-rich. Both mad for heroics. It makes a lot of sense. They met at the launch party for her rescue agency, didn't they? For the Caroliners? That's the first occasion for which there are photos of your mother and Truby together, at that nightclub in St Anton.'

They were questioning him. They hadn't yet hurt him – apart from the kick to his groin.

They needed him alive. Which meant that he had *time*.

Ben tried to concentrate on the sensation of his pulse against the tight plastic that bound his wrist. He tugged at the handcuff, allowing it to bite harder into his flesh. The pain was enough distraction to prevent him from releasing the anger that was building like a tide within. He clamped his jaw shut, forced himself to stare past Minos Winter and instead, to take in his surroundings. He'd been blindfolded, handcuffed in the car, led from the underground car park into which the Passat had been driven and into a cramped lift that had risen for at least four levels before opening directly into the lobby of an apartment.

Now he was tied to a wooden chair in the middle of an unfurnished room with a cherry-wood floor and plain white walls.

A sense of resignation assailed Ben. Two armed men against one unarmed boy, who was already bound to a chair. They'd taken his mobile phone from his jeans pocket the moment they'd walked through the door. They'd be able to get Truby's and Jasmine's mobile phone numbers from the device. Gemini Force One's number was filed under the label 'Dietz - work', but it wouldn't take anyone long to realise that 'Dietz - work' was the number he called most after Jasmine's and Truby's.

The situation looked worse by the minute. Winter's voice began to reach him again, although Ben realised he'd lost the thread somewhat. At the mention of his mother, it had been difficult to focus on anything other than the blinding anger that Winter's words provoked.

'Addison Nicole Dyer, am I right?'

Ben blinked a couple of times. He wasn't mistaken. Winter knew about Addison, too? His heart sank as he realised – Addison's connection with Caroline Carrington had almost certainly been established from the moment she'd been rescued by Caroline at the Sky High Hotel – an event that had been widely covered in the global press. Jason Truby had been there too. Yes – the moment that Winter had re-watched all those videos of the Sky High Hotel rescue and the press conference afterwards, it wouldn't have taken a genius to connect the four. Especially since a few months later they were in the news again – this time at the launch party for the Caroliners.

'Addison Dyer is *Aquarius*, yes?' Winter tilted Ben's chin with the muzzle of his SIG-Sauer pistol. 'Come on now, Carrington, just tell me.'

Ben locked eyes with Winter for a moment, allowed the full extent of his bitterness to permeate his gaze.

'Chill your boots, lad,' Winter murmured, lowering the gun to his side. 'The photos of Addison aren't as clear as the ones of you, but I'm pretty sure she's the pilot who was with you on *Macondo*. I'm guessing she's on the rather impressive aircraft that landed at the airfield a while ago.' Winter's lips twitched in amusement as he watched Ben struggle to contain his emotions. 'I hope so. I'm looking forward to seeing her again, too.'

Ben could feel himself beginning to tremble. He wasn't sure what was causing it – rage or fear?

Winter straightened up. He took a smart phone from his pocket. 'Let's hear what your friend Holden White has to say.'

On the screen of Winter's phone a video news clip was playing. Holden White, with a female protestor on either side of him, intensely earnest as he faced the interviewer.

'What you on about? I'm not going to stand here and tell you I think the Swiss police should use force to move these protestors. *Course* they shouldn't. Everyone in this human shield is a hero. You say it's spilling innocent blood, and all right, yeah, it might look like that. But sometimes even innocents have to be sacrificed for a noble cause. Like in the French Revolution – some innocent people died, but it was for the good of the people who went on to enjoy freedom.'

'Rock on, Holden,' Winter said quietly, his eyes on the phone screen.

A cold sweat broke out on Ben's back at the thoughts that struck him then. Could Holden White really be stupid enough to say such things without understanding the implications? What if he wasn't just mouthing off?

Had Holden White lured Ben into a trap?

THE SOUND OF FALLING

Ben finally managed to quell his trembling enough to ask a question of his own. 'Did you crash that plane into the Jungfraujoch tunnel?'

'That's enough from you. Now, here's where it gets unpleasant.'

From a pocket inside the black ski-suit, Minos Winter took a smooth black case, the kind that might contain reading glasses. But Ben recoiled when he saw what was inside - two plastic syringes and a glass vial that was half the size of his thumb.

Winter carefully broke the soft metal seal, removed the grey rubber stopper, then inserted the needle of one of the syringes, preparing the injection. The next time he looked at Ben it was with clinical detachment, sweeping his eyes across the boy's form as he evaluated the best way to deliver whatever was inside the syringe.

'Please,' Ben murmured, as Winter stepped towards him. He was totally helpless. That needle could be about to put anything into his bloodstream — a toxin that would paralyse him, or maybe some kind of truth serum to get him to talk about Gemini Force. Maybe something worse.

Winter, however, ignored the quiet plea for mercy. Ben clamped his jaw to prevent the humiliation of his teeth chattering. At least he could face his fate in silence. The cold steel of a needle sank into the muscle of his shoulder, exposed by the open flap of his jacket. To his faint surprise, Ben found that his last thought was not fear but resignation.

When he came to, Ben opened his eyes only to screw them shut again. A blinding white light engulfed him. His hands and feet were bound, he was slumped in the seat of a helicopter. A small one, to judge from the cramped space behind the pilot and co-pilot seats; little more than a glass bubble with a rotor blade and landing skids. Above, the weighty thrum of the rotor's blades made it impossible to hear what the pilot was saying into the radio.

Ben moved cautiously into an upright position. Warily, he peered into the front of the aircraft, where Minos Winter sat in the co-pilot seat. Below the chopper, a vista of jagged peaks and unspoilt, pure-white slopes drifted past. He kept his eyes half-closed as he tried to get his bearings, but it was impossible. How long had they been in the air? Were they still in Switzerland?

The helicopter lurched, plunged twenty metres in three seconds. The seatbelt dug into Ben's abdomen as he lifted off the seat. It dropped again, and again, in a series of clumsy jolts.

Minos Winter turned, lazily, in his seat. He gave Ben a thin smile. 'This is your stop, Carrington.'

Ben glared back, struggling against the cable ties that bound his wrists. They couldn't seriously mean to throw him out of the helicopter – could they? Winter pushed back his own seat, grabbed the door handle. A burst of freezing mist slapped Ben's face. He tried to gasp but it was as though all the air inside the helicopter had been instantly sucked away. Then Winter was leaning over the front seat, his right hand fumbling for the catch-release on Ben's seatbelt.

Ben threw all his weight onto the man's hand, pushing it away. A brick-hard knot of knuckles connected with his temple. A ringing sensation jolted between his ears, blurred his vision. He'd barely reacted when a second punch landed just above his right eye. He faltered, reeling and dizzy. When he could move again, icy sweat prickled his skin as Ben realised that his seat buckle had been unfastened.

The helicopter flew low over the mountains, so low that the crowns of tall fir trees almost scraped the landing skids. All thoughts of bravery escaped him, like air rushing from a burst balloon. Ben gulped down a breath, forced himself to focus on Winter. Whatever they had planned – and at this point he had to accept that it looked pretty grim – there seemed to be a short delay. Winter was studying something through the front window of the cockpit. Before Ben could follow his gaze, he felt Winter's fist clenching the front of his ski jacket. Then he was being dragged towards the open door, on the co-pilot side of the helicopter.

This time, Ben resisted for all he was worth. He braced both feet against the back of the pilot's seat, wedging himself into place as Winter continued to haul him along.

'Should have put him in the seat behind me like I told you!' Winter grunted. He pulled back a fist and slammed it into the boy. This time Ben's collar bone took the brunt of the strike. Juddering pain echoed through his entire torso. Falling forward, Ben's head caught the edge of the rear passenger seat, dangerously close to the open door of the helicopter.

Suddenly he was face to face with the wilderness below. The wind chill pricked at his eyes until they streamed with tears. His heart was thudding so hard against his ribs that he wondered if it might be a heart attack. And still the relentless drag of Winter's hands at his ski jacket, pulling and shoving until Ben's head and shoulders were hanging over the edge.

Pure terror raged in his blood. Ben's entire body felt as if he'd been electrocuted; tingling, the crackle of agony from the various blows he'd taken from Winter. His ears and the exposed skin of his face were bathed in a blast of freezing mist, the ferocious rustle of the wind in his hair. His eyes screwed up, self-preservation kicking in to protect him from the final sight that would await him as he surely fell to his death.

Then the final push, the shock of the drop. A distant

scream reached his ears. His own voice – the sound of falling.

He plunged head-first, a human torpedo. Ben's stomach slammed up against his diaphragm so hard that when he tried to draw breath, he couldn't. The hellish sensation of plummeting through the air didn't last, however. He'd barely registered that he had actually been thrust out of the helicopter when Ben felt an urgent tugging at his waist. Then he was jerking back upwards. He bounced, lightly, for a second or two before the direction changed.

Then once again, he was falling.

Ben's eyes snapped open. Wild with terror, he stared around him, below and above. His legs kicked, swinging freely, no longer bound. As his brain struggled to grasp the reality of hanging like a Christmas tree decoration from its branch, helplessly swept along by the helicopter above, Ben realised what must have happened. Winter must have sliced through the cable ties at the last moment before giving him the final push.

Focus returning, he noticed that the chopper was still flying in a straight line, dragging him through the air. Ben's hands were tied in front of him. Whatever was connecting him to the helicopter seemed to be fastened behind his back, to a belt around his waist.

About a hundred metres directly ahead, Ben spotted a tiny alpine hut – a wooden dwelling – the kind that hikers used for emergency shelter in storms. This one was perched close to the summit of a peak which rose above most of the smaller peaks in the vicinity. Above the tree line, it was obviously intended for serious climbers. There was no gentle slope connecting it to the nearest descent – only a sheer cliff wall.

The helicopter above was headed unswervingly for that isolated hut. Ben could feel his hands going numb, bitten by the cold. He could hardly see through the film of tears as his eyes reacted to the stinging wind. Every few seconds he remembered to breathe.

The peak that held the mountain hut filled his field of vision. Ben twisted on the end of the rope, looking up. He caught a glimpse of Winter, leaning out of the open door, yelling at Ben and pointing at the ground. Something flashed in his hand – the metal of a blade. Ben glanced down. He was right over the hut now, could almost touch it with his feet. Then he was falling again. It was over in a second. He sank immediately, up to his thighs in the deep powder.

The instant he hit the ground, Ben rolled to the right, spreading his weight and the impact of the drop. He flipped onto his back, gazing up after the helicopter. He'd fallen at least ten metres, buried hip-deep in snow. The rope from which he'd been suspended trailed from beneath him and lay in a disordered coil across the virgin snow between him and the mountain hut.

Ben's eyes closed for several seconds as he waited for his heart rate to come down. He forced himself to focus on each limb, moving it cautiously, anxious at any sign of pain. Yet as he sat up slowly inside the dent he'd made, it dawned on Ben that he'd reached the ground in one piece. The most immediate problem was the cold. If he didn't get inside that hut in the next few minutes, Ben knew that he wouldn't be able to move his fingers. And without fingers, it was pretty much game over.

In the next moment Ben was on his knees, crawling through the snow. Every time he tried to get enough leverage to stand, his hands sank through the fine surface snow, right up to the elbows. Lifting his feet out of the deep holes they'd made was slow work. Every step was an effort, but with a combination of crawling on knees and walking, he managed to drag himself through the snow drift to the door of the mountain hut. The door handle was an old, cast iron latch with a simple handle that pulled down to release the metal bar from its catch. Ben shivered with relief that it wasn't something more complicated. He pushed open the door and stepped inside along with the flurry of piled-up snow that collapsed when he moved the door.

With a heavy lean, the door closed behind him. Ben remained there for a moment, slowly aware that he was shaking with cold and fear. His fingers trembled with the effort of pulling down the zipper of his jacket. With his hands still bound by the plastic handcuffs, his most urgent job was to free them and warm himself up. Ben stuffed both hands into his left armpit. Cold surged into him as his body heat began to flow into his fingers.

Teeth chattering, he took in the rest of the hut. It was

a single room. A heavy metal wood burner stood in the middle of the room, with a chimney that led to the roof. He spotted a tiny box of matches next to a neat pile of tightly-rolled newspaper. Ben shuddered with relief – at least they didn't mean for him to die of cold. A two-man wooden bunk was in one corner of the room, made up with sheets, pillows and a feather quilt that just covered the mattress. The only light came from a single window in the wall opposite the door.

Still unsteady on his legs, Ben moved over to the wood burner. He dropped to his knees, suddenly aware that his trousers were quickly soaking up the dry snow with which they'd become thickly coated outside. Reluctantly, he pulled his hands out from the warmth under his arms and used his wrists to brush away as much snow as he could.

Warm and dry. It had to be his top priority.

Shivering, he began to strike matches. He held one beneath the plastic of the cable tie on his left hand until he was chewing on his lip, whimpering from the pain of burning flesh as the plastic began to melt against his skin. In another few seconds the ordeal was over. Ben pressed lumps of compacted snow against his wrists to soothe his burns, and turned his attention to making a fire.

The wood burner had been neatly stacked with wedges of dry pine wood, as well as interleaved with tightly rolled newspaper pages, the size of cigars. It didn't take long before flames were licking over the wood. He closed the stove's little window and for several moments, he simply watched the fire dancing behind the glass. Then he placed his hands on the heavy wrought iron casing of the wood burner, closed his eyes, panting slightly as he felt heat seeping through his palms, and sensation returning to his fingers.

When he felt a little better, Ben unzipped his jacket pockets, carefully removing each item inside. Laid out on the tarnished, antique pine floor before him were all his available assets.

His mobile phone. It was still almost fully charged, but he wasn't remotely surprised to find there was no signal. Of course not. They'd never allow him to call for help.

Two discs of lemongrass-scented soap, wrapped in waxed paper. A vial of lemongrass and vanilla body lotion. A shoe shine set. A sewing kit. A polythene bag containing twelve squares of four varieties of Cailler milk chocolate. A tiny box of small matches. A gingerbread-scented candle in a shot glass. Three tiny glass vials, samples of cologne.

It wasn't much of a survival kit – probably the reason that they'd left the items in his pockets. Ben unwrapped a piece of chocolate and popped it into his mouth – amazed as ever at how soothing it was under tough conditions. Like instant hope.

He knew enough about the mountains to know that his best chance of survival was to stay put, where he was warm. He stood, began to look more closely around the hut. Behind the wood burner was a shovel – presumably for clearing snow away from the door, and an aluminium bucket. There was no sign of water, but the bucket, Ben realised quickly, would hold about two litres of snow that would melt down, if he placed it somewhere hot.

Nervously, he peered into the shadows in the upper-reaches of the hut. Something about those dark spaces made his skin crawl. He used a match to light his scented candle, and raised it towards the sloping ceiling for a better look. Almost immediately, he dropped the candle. His pulse thundered in his own ears as he fell to the ground, reclaiming the candle. When he looked at the ceiling again, he was breathless. Yet there it was - no mistaking it.

An object the size and shape of a bar of butter, with two short metal sticks poking out of it, wired to a smart phone that was also attached to the ceiling.

Plastic explosives; C4 at a guess. Wired to a detonator. The wires led to a mobile phone. Ben swallowed, tried to breathe. The detonator would be wirelessly operated. Probably a radio signal. He released a long breath. His thoughts grew more disordered by the second. Distinct, cold-edged panic was sliding into him.

Ben was trapped inside a totally isolated mountain hut, wired with explosives. He could guess who had control of the detonator. But why?

He reached, almost automatically, for his own mobile phone. Maybe if he hunted for a signal? But there was no spot inside that hut where he could receive anything from the outside world.

Then he noticed that a video-playing app was open. A touch of his fingertip brought that app to the foreground. He didn't recognise the image on the screen. It wasn't a video he'd made. With feelings of trepidation, he touched the play button.

On the phone's screen, a snowy landscape cleared – the lens was zooming in, fast. It stopped when the image of a solitary mountain hut filled the screen.

'This is where we're holding Count Benedict Carrington. We prepared it especially for him. He'll be warm and comfortable. He can melt snow to drink.'

Ben didn't recognise the voice, which had been electronically modified. The image changed – now the screen was showing the inside of the hut. The camera swept across the bed, to the wood-burning stove and then up to the sloping wooden ceiling. It stopped when it had focused on the very thing at which Ben had just been staring – the explosive device.

'This is our little IED. Ben would be ill-advised to attempt to dismantle it, unless his training has included some advanced bomb disposal techniques. At nine am tomorrow morning, the device will stop receiving radio signals from me. At nine am tomorrow morning, this device will cease to be a danger to Ben.'

There was a heavy pause.

'All you have to do between now and nine am tomorrow is this: nothing. Do not attempt to rescue the trapped delegates. Respect our circle of protection. Let fate play its card. The game of capitalism is rigged.

This cannot be tolerated. We need a new game.'

Then the image onscreen was of the hut again, from the outside, the frame shaking enough that Ben guessed it was probably being viewed through a powerful telephoto lens.

Whoever had filmed this wasn't too far from where he was. The image was a stark reminder that there was no way off the ledge on which the hut was built; not without rock climbing equipment. Then the voice - a rasping, metallic sound – spoke once again.

'For the sake of billions of people who can never get their fair share, we need to end the current game. Leave the delegates where they are. Let the world see that advantage comes at a deadly price. We recognise that these people have committed no legal crime. The real crime is a system that allows them to prosper. The system itself must be dismantled. With the deaths of the delegates, others will understand that to take advantage of an evil system now puts them at risk. We repeat - leave the delegates where they are. For twenty hours. Or Benedict Carrington will die.'

The image of the dreary little alpine hut began to fade to black. In its place appeared the hashtag: #NEWGAME

← INSTRUCTIONS ←

It was like some kind of insane, revolting practical joke. At first, Ben seethed with outrage. The feeling didn't last. The stark reality of his surroundings, the sound of the high-altitude wind against the flimsy wooden walls of the hut, the last vestiges of cold burning his fingers; each thing confirmed the danger of his situation.

It was almost one o'clock in the afternoon. The first avalanche had struck at around eight-thirty in the morning. The trapped conference delegates had around nineteen-and-a-half hours of air left, according to Ben's recollection. They were, effectively, hostages in the process of being buried alive. This meant that there were well under twenty hours during which action had to be taken. Realistically though, it would take several hours to locate and dig them out. Ben remembered hearing Dietz say something about four hours, to be safe. Gemini Force safety margins were generous. At a push, they could do the job in half the time.

Which meant that a rescue effort would have to begin by 4.30 a.m. the next day, to have even a small chance of success.

Terrorists. There was no other way to describe Winter and his group. #NEWGAME was all about starting over, creating some new kind of political and economic system for the world. A fairer system, probably. His mother's words returned to him.

If things were fair, Ben, we'd be poor.

Ben had no idea how the system could be changed, or even if it were possible. But a deep, powerful instinct told him that if it took violence, if it required the death of innocents, then what #NEWGAME was doing had to be wrong.

Especially if one of those innocents was him.

Perched on the lower bunk bed, Ben tried to calm himself. It was impossible.

How dare they? How dare they trick Holden White into being a mouthpiece for their twisted ideas? How dare they use an idealistic rock star to lure a sixteen-year-old to his potential death? How dare they use the protective feelings of Jason Truby towards the youngest member of his team, asking him to value Ben's life more highly than the delegates'?

It took Ben several more minutes to absorb the possible outcome.

What if Jason chose to save the delegates? But then again, what if Jason Truby gave in, agreed to hold Gemini Force back from this rescue, if he traded Ben's life for all those hostages?

It would mean that no member of Gemini Force could ever feel safe again. All anyone would need to do would be to capture one of them, threaten violence, and Truby's hand would be stayed.

By now, Truby had probably seen the #NEWGAME video message. Truby would think it over for a while; discuss things with Dietz, maybe James and Nina too. Then he'd decide. If he decided to send in Gemini Force, Ben could expect the C4 to be detonated any time.

A trickle of fear ran along Ben's spine. He had *no* idea how much time he had.

He pushed back, mentally, forced the fear out of his mind for a moment, tried to focus on what he could actually do. It wasn't easy. He felt short of breath, unsteady as his heart rate continued to soar.

The damp, stale and bitterly cold air inside the hut was being overtaken, gradually, with warmth. As the scent of burning pine reached his nose, for just a moment, Ben was overtaken with the thought that it could all end here. Alone, at the summit of an alpine mountain, thick blankets of snow outside, soft flakes whipping through the wind as it snaked around the hut. Sheltered at least, cosy and infused with the comforting aroma of wood smoke. It wouldn't be the worst way to die. He probably wouldn't even live long enough to hear the explosion, let alone experience the sensation of being ripped apart. A quicker death than either of his parents.

Yet - why should the Carrington family be wiped out? Why should Jasmine have to go through losing him – even before they were properly together? Ben couldn't allow it to happen. Somehow, he had to get a grip. Fear was a luxury. He might have hours left. He might have minutes. He had to make each one count.

And once he'd calmed a little, he accepted that there was only one solution. Ben had to get out of the hut and get a message to Gemini Force.

As soon as they knew he was safely out of the hut, Winter would cease to have any threat to hold over them and the rescue could begin.

For a moment he almost laughed at the sheer impossibility of this notion. Sure. He was getting out of here without skis, without any kind of survival equipment. He was getting off a sheer mountain peak. *Right.*

Except . . . Ben began to wonder. *Why not?* If he stayed in the hut, there was an excellent chance that he'd be blown up. It might even happen soon. Surely anything was better than just sitting here, waiting to be torn apart by a bomb.

With a twinge of despair, Ben realised it might be easier to set the bomb off deliberately, rather than do nothing. If Truby saw the mountain hut explode, he'd definitely start the rescue. You didn't even hear the explosion when you were this close to a bomb; that's what he'd heard. Your ability to hear was destroyed roughly the same time that the sound of the explosion reached your ears. He could probably psych himself up to it, thinking of all the lives he'd save.

Giving up though? That went against every impulse. On balance, he preferred to die trying to escape.

OK then – self-rescue it is. How do I start?

If only he had Internet access, he'd at least have a chance to find instructions for disarming an IED. This thought brought the first touch of a grin to Ben's lips. That would take real nerve – using bomb disposal instructions you found on the Internet to save your own life. Would he even have the guts to try? It almost made him glad that it couldn't be put to the test.

Except . . .

And an idea came to him. A preposterously bold idea.

Ben looked down. Beneath him, a white cotton duvet covered a thin mattress. He stood, lifting the mattress to examine the base. It was made of pine slats, each one about a metre and a half in length.

Disposing of a bomb would be scary. Failure would be met with swift punishment. Yet the idea that was slowly occurring to Ben wasn't a lot safer, or easier.

He plucked at the quilt, dragged it from the bed and stripped off its cover. One hundred per cent cotton. He tugged at the sheet that covered the mattress. Lightweight yet sturdy, woven cotton. He pulled the sheet between outstretched arms, mentally calculating the length. He dropped the sheet on the top bunk and looked at the neatly arranged pile of assets that he'd filched from the hotel suite.

This might just be possible.

He paced over to the wood burner in the centre of the room. He'd left his phone on the floor. He was about to pick it up when it struck Ben that if he planned on drinking anything in the next few hours – and he had to admit, swallowing a new wave of terror, that it would take a few hours – then he'd need to start melting some snow.

He went to the door, opened it and used the metal bucket to catch the snow that fell. He closed the door again – it really was hideously cold out there – and placed the bucket of snow on top of the stove. It just about fitted, jammed up against the chimney pipe.

Then he looked at his phone. No Internet access was needed to find the document he'd downloaded earlier – the parasailing instructions. If he'd remembered correctly, there was a detailed diagram of a parasail.

With no rock-climbing gear, he was trapped on this mountain peak. But maybe he could *fly* to freedom.

After a few moments scrutinising the diagram, Ben stripped down the upper bunk. He laid the bedding on the floor, then sat, cross-legged, and opened the sewing kit. It was one of the best he'd ever seen – as good as the ones that Carrington International had once provided for their hotel guests. The scissors were sharp and had one pointed tip – perfect for making holes for threading. Needles of a wide variety, presented in a smart plastic carousel, measuring tape and even a chunk of blue chalk. There were six bobbins of thread – the ones with black and white thread were twice the size of the other colours.

Ben concentrated on the diagram of the parasail again. He calculated that he'd need twenty strips of fabric, each roughly twenty-five centimetres wide and up to two metres long to make the canopy. The first task was to cut these out of the sheets and the duvet covers, and sew them together. While he was doing that he could start to worry about what he was going to use for risers; the long, sturdy strings that would connect him to the canopy. The sewing thread obviously wouldn't be enough. But maybe the woven silk in his scarf? Silk, after all, was famous for having incredible tensile strength. It was what commercial parasails used.

Ben threaded a finger into the knot of the silk scarf that Truby had given him, slowly pulled it free of his neck. This whole situation must be a nightmare for Truby. The more he got to know him, the more Ben began to suspect that things had gotten pretty serious between his mother and Truby.

Whatever the guy had promised Caroline about Ben's future, it obviously carried a lot of weight in his heart. Now he was being forced to actually consider letting Ben die. A rough deal, no doubt at all.

Ben ran the tips of his fingers along the fine loose strands at each end of the scarf, considering. He could tear and cut the scarf into long, narrow strips.

Finally, he could feel a sense of purpose returning; felt the dread and panic subside. This was a plan. He'd have to work hard, steady and precise with the needle and thread, a critical eye on the design at every stage. There would be no time, no room for fear and doubt. Every single cell of his mind and body would need to be dedicated to the task. Not just to fashioning some equipment to help him get off the peak, but to survive the mountain once he was free.

His fingers made a fist in the cool cotton of the duvet cover, clutching tightly at the fabric that might save him. It would be unbelievably makeshift. But the parasail would only have to be good enough to be used once.

One wild ride off the edge of a mountain and into the dazzling white beyond.

‒ VERTICAL DEATH ‒

It took Ben two hours to construct half of the parasail's canopy. The whole time, the explosive device sat like some gigantic poisonous spider lurking in the recesses of the ceiling. An omnipresent itch of uneasiness scarcely left him, but after a while Ben recognised that there was something extraordinarily soothing about the rhythmic movement of thread through fingers, of needle through cotton. His motions were deeply repetitive, mesmerising. There was comfort, too in the faint crackle of the wood in the burner, the smell of burning pine. Once Ben had relaxed enough to get into the rhythm of it, the work moved much faster. After another fifty minutes, he'd completed the parasail. Lacking a harness, he'd painstakingly sewn the risers directly into his jacket. He planned on taking everything with him, including the scissors, so when he landed, he'd simply slice through the risers to remove the canopy.

He drank some meltwater from the metal bucket he'd placed on the stove, wiped his mouth with the sleeve of his cashmere sweater. Almost ready.

Unless ‒ dare he risk it? Ben couldn't help feeling that some kind of skis would be better than nothing, in the event that he made it off the peak. Would it be possible to make skis from the wooden slats of the bunk beds? He picked up the shovel from where it lay, untouched, beside the stove.

He removed the mattress of the lower bunk, then braced one foot in the corner of the bed frame, before wedging the metal edge of the shovel between one of the cross-slats. The first slat snapped clean across, splintering badly. Useless. He tried again, with the next slat. It was even more tightly glued into place, and cracked audibly as he bore down on it. The third slat, however, lifted off almost cleanly, as though it had barely been touched by the adhesive that kept most of the cheap bed frame together.

Ben held the piece of wood in his hand. It would make a very short ski – only a metre and a half. But at a pinch, especially if he used the soap to wax the base of each slat, he might be able to ski on it. There were plenty of off-cuts from the sheets that he could use to bind his hiking boots to the wood. No quick-release metal binding, but then again, hadn't he heard countless stories of his grandfather's heroic skiing exploits, long before ski equipment had become so fancy? Now was Ben's own chance to prove himself a true heir to the Brandis family name. Mountains were their domain.

After another thirty minutes he was standing on the pine wood skis, stamping both feet up and down inside the hut to check how tightly the bindings held him to the wooden slats. The hut smelled like lemongrass now; he'd rubbed the best part of a cake of soap over the underside of his improvised skis before he'd attached them to his feet.

Almost ready.

Now that the moment was approaching, Ben's former urgency had drained away. He found himself making excuses to stay a little longer. He'd spent at least ten minutes simply re-filling his jacket pockets, placing the shovel by the door so that he could grab it on his way out.

Every single item might help him survive. A shovel could build a snow cave. It was four-thirty in the afternoon, according to his phone. Less than an hour of light left. And even if there was moonlight, Ben knew that he'd never survive outside of a snow cave, not at night, when temperatures could drop to minus twenty degrees Celsius.

Soon enough though, there was nothing left to be done. Only waiting to be blown up.

It had taken him three and a half hours to get into a position where escape was possible. As much as a knot of pure fear remained coiled in his belly, they hadn't been the worst hours of his life. If they were to be his last, Ben suspected that the only better way to spend them would be if he was using every minute directly to save someone else's life. Since he couldn't dig those people out himself, this was the only way to save them.

Ben zipped his mobile phone into his inside jacket pocket, removing his thin leather gloves. They'd at least provide some protection against the chill. But he was going to have to keep his hands in his pockets wherever possible.

He ate another piece of chocolate washed down with the remaining litre of meltwater. Who knew when he'd next be able to drink? Ben picked up his jacket, now heavy with the added weight of the parasail to which it was attached. He slipped it over his shoulders then hooked the empty bucket over one arm so that he could take that, too.

With one final, wary glance at the IED in the corner of the hut, Ben moved towards the door, the parasail draped with utmost care over his right arm. The idea that the bomb might go off any minute now surged back into his consciousness.

At the last moment, Ben remembered that his captors had a telephoto lens trained on the hut. He'd seen the door of the hut in the image that had been shown on the video message they'd left for him. They might be close enough to recapture him. He'd have to leave via the window.

As long as he could get to somewhere with a phone signal, he'd put his money on Gemini Force reaching him before Minos Winter and his cronies.

He placed one hand on the window latch, and pushed it open.

Most likely the jump's going to kill me.

There it was. He'd admitted it to himself – his worst fear. And now that he'd faced it, he pushed his shoulders back inside his jacket.

Oh well. Who wants to live for ever?

With that, he climbed awkwardly through the window, then dragged the canopy through after him, into the bright white outside. The makeshift skis made an immediate improvement from when he'd been outside before, dragging his feet through a snowdrift. Now he was cutting through the powder pile – slowly, but with so much less effort. On this side of the hut, the slope was gentle, until it reached a sheer drop – the cliff face that climbers relished as the final stage of their route to this hut.

Ben approached the drop-off, sliding almost lazily towards oblivion. He bent his knees, shifted his weight forwards, willing the descent. Beyond the edge he could see thin wisps of cloud wrapping through the air. Far, very far below, the pristine slopes of the mountain lead to the valley below.

He might be crushed on impact. But then again, wasn't that always the risk?

I can do this.

A vast expanse of empty air filled his horizon. The canopy was still dragging, uselessly, along the surface of the snow. A proper parasail would have lifted by now. Like a feather in a light breeze, it would have wafted up behind him until he felt the risers pull tight and lift him off the ground. But his all-cotton canopy just wasn't light enough. It would take the full force of an upwards blast of air to fill it. Sickeningly, Ben realised that he'd feel the fall, a genuinely terrifying plunge through nothingness, until the canopy would function as a parasail. He'd have to be rushing through the air at a terrifying speed to get all that cotton and thread to bloom into the arc of a parasail and save him from being smashed on the limestone rocks below.

Two metres from the edge. One metre. Centimetres away. His eyes glazed as he stared over the edge, as death approached; pure, vertical death.

Hello, Sky High Hotel.

The improvised skis tipped over the edge, pitched him forwards. Then he was face to face with the drop. A wall of grey limestone glowed pale pink in the rays of the afternoon light. It was the last thing Ben saw rush past him before his eyes scrunched up, unable to watch any more.

Falling. Again.

━ AIRBORNE ━

He managed to fall feet first. Headfirst and he would probably somersault, roll himself like a pancake inside the canopy, slice through the air like a freshly-wrapped Egyptian mummy and wind up being compressed into a bloody mess somewhere down the slope.

Feet first, Ben might have a shot at surviving long enough to speed ride.

The sensation of falling was mind-meltingly hideous. As though a monstrous vacuum were trying to remove his organs and blood through the soles of his feet. Panic burst like white blindness behind his eyelids. Just when he felt like his chest and head might explode from the intensity of it all, Ben felt the violent tug of the silk risers he'd sewn into his jacket. The sudden deceleration was like being hauled backwards through a tornado, the sound of wind flapping through cotton roaring in his ears. Ben's muscles, tense to the point of rigidity, relaxed very slightly as he waited for the start of something more pleasant – the heady sensation of speed riding.

It never came. His blissful moment of relaxation simply blinked out of existence as Ben grasped the truth.

The canopy *had* ballooned open over him, he was hanging from the risers, parasailing down the mountain, but *still* he was falling much too fast. In desperation, Ben reached behind his right shoulder, clutched at a handful of risers. Abruptly, the parasail swerved to the right and dipped. It began to corkscrew, spinning him so fast that he couldn't focus on anything.

He was totally out of control, careening towards the white expanse of the lower slopes. With less than three seconds before he hit the ground, Ben pulled both knees tight to his chest and tucked in his arms. As the ground rushed up to meet him, he felt his improvised skis splinter as they took the brunt of the impact. He felt the crunch of bones and an explosion of pain as kneecaps slammed into his chin and ribs. Instinctively, both arms reached out to wrap tightly around Ben's shoulders as his weight toppled forwards. A compact human cannonball rolled down the mountain, tangled up in a net of silk and cotton. He went head over heels five times before coming to a halt.

For the first two minutes, Ben didn't move at all, hardly dared to breathe. The sheer fact that he was able to breathe at all came as such a relief that he felt like shouting with joy. The relief, however, was short-lived. Various parts of his body were registering pain, and his heart was pounding so violently against aching ribs that he couldn't quite tell where any injury might be, at first. But as he slowly unwound his limbs, it became strikingly clear. A steady pulse of agony blazed in his right foot.

With a loud groan, Ben fell back against the snow.

That's when he first noticed that he'd somehow lost the glove from his left hand. He spread both arms wide, experimentally shifting his left leg, then his right. His right ankle felt like it was being consumed by fire. The pain was intensifying fast enough that within five minutes Ben had pushed himself into a sitting position and was frantically tugging at the laces of his hiking boots, bursting to get something cold to that furnace of pain. A moment later, his foot was free of the boot. Wincing, Ben peeled the sock off a rapidly swelling ankle and then plunged bare skin into a fluffy pile of dry snow.

As the cold began to numb the pain, Ben leaned back, trailing gloved fingers through deep, loose powder. Breathing tightly, he forced himself to experiment with the full range of movement of his right foot. Pain erupted in his ankle. He bit down on his lower lip to stop it from trembling. He could scarcely move the foot at all. His ankle was almost certainly broken.

He took another moment to steady his breathing. Light flakes of snow fell onto his eyelids and cheeks. He felt them melt like frozen tears. Slowly, he opened his eyes, allowed himself to take in a more detailed view of his surroundings.

A sheer cliff face loomed overhead, a backdrop to the gentler slope that began somewhere behind him. Below, the slope narrowed to a gulley between two smaller mounds, each one between fifteen and twenty metres high. Beyond that, all he saw was the dark mass of trees – a wood of tall fir trees that stretched for at least half a kilometre in every direction.

He clasped a hand to the front of his jacket, fumbling with the zip. After a frustrating few seconds, he pulled the glove away, opened his jacket and reached inside for his mobile phone. Holding onto a breath, he brought the screen in front of his face. The phone signal icon was empty. Ben's eyes slammed shut. Disappointment clutched at his chest - harder than he'd expected.

Of course there was no signal all the way out here. He blinked away the film of tears that had formed and swept the horizon for any sign of a telecoms mast. There it was, in the distance, maybe ten kilometres east of his current position. The mast was mounted on a minor summit in a cluster of peaks that Ben guessed were at elevations of between one thousand and fifteen hundred metres.

All he had to do was get close enough. Then he could call Gemini Force. They'd start rescuing the delegates. And they'd rescue him. Five kilometres might get him within range. Maybe less.

Just walk.

His ankle was broken. The wooden slats that he'd used as skis had snapped and left stumps of splintered pine attached to his boots. And now, Ben slowly registered that somewhere on the fall, he'd let go of the shovel. The only thing he could have used as a crutch – and it was gone.

Ben collapsed, let himself fall onto his back, arms

outstretched. A laugh began to overtake him; a despairing, ironic laugh. It wasn't long before he began to feel the chill of deep snow beneath his legs. During an Alpine winter it was good sense to wear thermal long johns whenever outside, but since living in the Caribbean, at GF One, Ben wasn't always so careful. It had been sheer luck that he'd worn them today. The tough physical regime of being part of Gemini Force was altering the shape of his body and the trousers he was wearing, warm moleskin jeans, hung loose on his hips unless he added the extra layer of thermals.

In the wilderness, a small detail like that could save your life. A sobering thought. If he managed to collect up every one of the small details in his favour, Ben thought, he might yet get out of this alive.

He struggled to his feet, brushing snow from the backs of his thighs with his one gloved hand. The exposed left hand, he tucked underneath his jacket and into his armpit. Losing heat from his core was a bad idea when there was no obvious way to restore it.

But frozen fingers and feet would kill him even faster.

⟞ SMALL DETAILS ⟝

Ben couldn't tell whether he'd broken the ankle or merely sprained it, but the pain was already insistent enough to be a drain on his energy. His next task had to be getting his injured right foot back into the boot. He'd iced the ankle; hopefully that had reduced some of the swelling. Rest should have been the next treatment – not exactly an option right now. Yelps of agony escaped him over the next few moments as he struggled to roll his sock over his foot and then stuff it back into the boot.

When the job was done, Ben was breathing with a jagged, uneven rhythm. Still unsteady on his feet, he used the sewing kit scissors to sever each one of the risers that connected the canopy of the parasail to his jacket. After a moment's consideration he tore some of the cotton into strips, removed his jacket, and wrapped a strip of sheet around his head, then around his torso, tying the tapered ends in a granny knot. Gingerly, he replaced his jacket, and sucked in his breath as he forced the zipper closed. Now his ears were neatly tucked under the thick layer of cotton and his chest felt comfortably tight beneath the jacket. At least he would freeze to death a lot more slowly.

Time was the single crucial factor, now. It was coming up to 4.45 p.m.: over four hours since Minos Winter had dumped him at the summit. Ben had calculated that if Truby planned to let the terrorists influence him at all, he'd at least give Ben a few hours to escape before he risked a rescue of the buried VIPs. The fact that the mountain hut hadn't yet been blown up meant that so far, no rescue had begun. Truby might wait a little longer, but the sooner that Ben could get word to him that he wasn't in the hut any more, the more chance that they could get the delegates out.

Another, chilling possibility was that Truby wasn't prepared to risk Ben's life at all. That could turn Ben into the indirect cause of a lot of deaths. He couldn't allow that. Reflexively, he glanced up at the summit. From this angle, he couldn't see the mountain hut.

Please, explode.

Until the hut blew up, he hadn't won. Ben's own survival wasn't even required for victory. Not today, at least. All he needed was to know that no one would die because of him. One little fireball – was it too much to ask? But there was nothing but the whispering echo of an Alpine breeze across a limestone wall, where the sunset made the rocks glow the colour of peach roses.

Ben turned his attention to finding his left glove and shovel. He'd dropped both, as well as the bucket, the instant he'd hit the ground. It had been ambitious, hoping to hang on to everything. Now, he had no choice. He had to retrieve that shovel. If he could tightly bind its handle to his ankle, it would be a workable crutch. He took his mobile phone from his zipped jacket pocket and checked the time again.

The sky was pretty clear, which meant that he could count on another half-hour or so of russet lighting as the sun set. He scoured his memory for any clue about the phase of the moon. It had been overcast at night for days, however – he couldn't remember when he'd last seen the moon. Ben faced the sky, hopefully. If it stayed clear tonight, the cold would be brutal. But a decent moon would guide his way, reflecting the pure white of the slope. One more small detail that might tip things in his favour.

He had maybe an hour to make as much progress as he could. Ben could only hope and pray that it would be far enough to bring him within the signal of the nearest transmission tower. Then he could alert Gemini Force. If nothing else, it would free Truby of the threat posed by #NEWGAME.

The trick would be to do it before he dropped dead of cold. Ben found himself chuckling once again at the situation. The only help he could offer those buried hostages was to save himself.

Ben's eyes narrowed, scouring the landscape nearby for the discarded shovel. After several minutes of patient scrutiny, he caught sight of a strange shadow that stretched beneath a swell in the snow. If he squinted, it might just be the elongated shape of the shovel's blade. He lowered himself carefully onto his hands and began to make his way across the slope, moving like a three-legged dog. So long as his injured foot didn't take any weight, the pain was bearable. Within five minutes he'd found the shovel. It was mostly buried by snow, with just the tip of the spade protruding.

He set about the business of binding his right leg to the shovel. Placing the shoulder of the blade flush against his hip, he tied the handle to his injured foot. He used four of the risers cut from his jacket to ensure that the limb had absolutely no freedom of movement.

It was time he got moving. But still no sign of his second glove.

Ben transferred the contents of his left jacket pocket (a plastic bag containing squares of milk chocolate) to his right pocket, unwrapped two squares and placed one chocolate into each cheek, then stuffed his cold-chapped hand into the empty, fleece-lined pouch.

The sweetness and faintly caramelised milk flavour of the Cailler chocolate flowed through Ben, a wave of comfort. He oriented himself with the distant telecommunications mast, and began to walk towards it.

The light was failing fast; even the snow was turning the colour of a blush. When occasionally Ben checked over his shoulder for glimpses of the mountain hut, he noticed his own shadow lengthening across the snow. The dimples of his footprints deepened in shade, appearing ominously like the trail of some enormous Yeti in steady pursuit.

Try as he might, it was impossible to wholly keep his

weight off his injured foot. With his left hand tucked against his body, a fist clenched inside the pocket of his jacket, his balance wasn't what it needed to be. He longed to remove the hand, but forced himself to put up with the ungainly gait of his progress. If rescue didn't come very soon, Ben would need *both* his hands to have any chance of staying alive.

Every few steps he'd unavoidably lean to the right and then wince or even shout out a curse as a bolt of pain shot through him, like a blunt nail being hammered upwards into the bone. Despite the cold, Ben could feel sweat pouring from his head and down his back. It was the sweat of desperation and fear.

He was moving too slowly.

Ben stalled, his lungs dragging in more air. He couldn't rip his gaze away from the distant transmission tower. It would soon be dark, too dark for straining eyes to make out a safe path down the slope. He stopped, stood absolutely still and focused on the sounds of the air, hoping desperately for the distant hum of helicopter blades. But, nothing.

He took out his mobile phone. Thirty percent of the battery power remained. Still no phone signal.

There was a deep ache inside his chest, as though he'd been hollowed out. Tears of frustration stung the cold, drying surface of his eyeballs.

It's right there!

Pain reverberated, a steady pulse through his right leg. Another ache was invading him, he could feel it

– duller, yet more dangerous. The cold. His leg muscles throbbed with an iciness that was reaching, slowly and deeply, into his bones.

A lone silhouette on a slope of pristine powder, Ben cast a frantic gaze towards the woods between him and the telecoms mast. In the woods, he might have a chance at surviving the night. But there was no possible way he'd reach the trees before darkness fell.

For the past few hours, hope had been simmering within his heart. As the final rays of light burned their shadows onto the winter wilderness, Ben forced himself to face the truth.

Somehow, he'd managed to escape without #NEWGAME realising. Winter was still playing chicken with Truby. Unless Ben could get a signal to him, to let him know he was alive and out of the hut, the rescue would not begin.

Minos Winter would have won.

~ SNOW HOLE ~

Every instinct told Ben to keep moving. To stop now felt like lying down to die. If he kept going, at least he'd be doing something when death came, he'd be fighting it. Maybe you didn't feel death so badly, if you were fighting right to the end.

Yet some part of his brain, cornered off from the rest of his mind, was telling him that his strategy had to change. No more dashing ahead, racing for the chance to contact Gemini Force and let them know he was no longer in the hut. The sun had set now and it was getting dark. The temperature was dropping fast. Ben had to find a way to get warm and play for time.

He'd ignored that part of himself until now. But as the sunlight disappeared, he stood knee-deep in snow and felt the cold trying to claim the lower half of his body. A survival response must have kicked in. Finally, he was listening to that inner voice.

He had to use the last of his energy to build a snow cave. The night would get brutally, lethally cold. He *had* to take shelter now, rather than risk the last of his strength to reach the woods.

Caroline Carrington had taken Ben for his first overnight winter hike when he was just twelve years old. Her own father had done the same for her when she was twelve.

'A Brandis has to be tough,' she'd told him with a smile. 'But don't worry. We're not Spartans. I'm not going to abandon you.'

They'd ended up losing their tent – Ben's mistake, one that Caroline had never mentioned again. They'd improvised a shelter by using a hand saw from her backpack to carve wedges of snow and remove blocks with their hands.

Ben stooped to untie the bindings that strapped the shovel to his right leg and boot. His foot was so cold now that he could barely feel the pain of the break. But the moment he put weight onto the unsupported foot, bolts of agony shot into him. Leaning all his weight onto his left leg, Ben began to dig out chunks of snow. Over the next fifteen minutes he dug out a hole that reached his elbow. He scraped the blade of the shovel against that single face, now sheltered from the wind. Despite the torment of relentless pain, he worked hard. The cold scared him more than the dark, which was surprisingly slow in descending fully. The sky remained a shade of dark blue several short of the velvet black of true night, against the pale glow of the snow. At the edge of the sky Ben detected a faint, greenish glow.

The moon. It had to be on its way over the mountain. It looked close to being full. Hope flared inside him and he threw his shoulder into the work of carving an upside-down L-shape into the snow face he'd created.

The vertical part of the 'L' was just narrow enough for him to slide into, side-on. The horizontal part, once he began working on it, was twice as deep as his chest. Once he'd made it large enough, he experimented with rolling onto the ledge he'd created. It wasn't quite long enough for him to lie at full stretch, but he was in a rush to stop working and get inside, where it was already several degrees warmer than out.

It was so dark inside the snow cave that he could barely see his hand in front of him. But he didn't need to see to be able to scratch a second ledge, rougher and much shallower, on the other side of the narrow vertical opening to the shelter. With his teeth, he pulled his right hand free of the glove. Rummaging in his pocket with his right hand, Ben placed the shot glass containing the candle on the ledge opposite. He reached back into the pocket, removed the box of matches. With the immobile claw of his uncovered hand, he held the box open as with his right hand he pulled out and then struck a match and lit the candle.

For a few minutes he simply held his frozen fingers as close to the flame as he dared, gasping as the blood began to circulate once again, flushing tingles of electricity through each digit. His tiny, enclosed shelter glowed orange. A shadow of the single flame danced, the movement almost hypnotic.

Ben wasn't sure how much time had gone by when his focus returned. He could move the individual fingers of his left hand again, although they still hurt. With clumsy movements, he managed to transfer the glove to his left hand. His right hand wasn't massively better off, but the thin leather had been better than nothing. He listened to the sound of his own breathing and felt the static clearing from his mind.

Two more things to do before he could rest.

Ben moved the candle to the ledge on which he'd be sleeping, then wedged his right elbow into the gap. Using three fingers as a drill, he bored a vertical hole into the snow. It would act as a chimney. After a few minutes his arm was buried to the shoulder in the snow and his fingers still hadn't found the outside. Ben shuffled, levered his arm into the ceiling of snow. Grunting with effort, he forced his hand even higher until at last, he felt the snap of freezing wind on his fingertips. Withdrawing his arm, he replaced the candle on the ledge just below the chimney. Now he wouldn't suffocate.

One thing left to do. It was by far the hardest. Ben sighed as he picked up the shovel, then turned sideways to wriggle out of the shelter. He took out his mobile phone and activated the distress signal app that Dietz had created for all members of the team. He checked the time – 6.34 p.m. Out of range of the telecoms mast, his phone was silent. But if he could just get it close enough . . .

He placed the phone on the shovel's blade, then rested the shaft lightly on his shoulder, pointing his body towards the transmission tower.

In lacrosse practice at Kenton College, where he'd been at school since the age of thirteen, Ben had once used the stick to hurl a ball almost three hundred and fifty metres. It was a long way short of the world record, but compared well for boys his age.

If he could throw his phone even three hundred metres . . . It would be that much closer to the transmission tower. It could make all the difference.

He'd be totally cut off, without any further chance to communicate. But truthfully, how much worse off would he actually be? At this point, a dead mobile phone was as much use to him as a live one.

Ben took a heavy breath, climbed out of the snow hole he'd dug and prepared to put his whole body into the swing. The he leaned back and whipped the shovel through the air. The phone flew off, unseen and unheard against the night sky.

He turned to the mountain, frowning up at the summit. The silvery haze behind the craggy peaks confirmed what he'd hoped – the moon was definitely on its way. He could just make out the outline of the hut – still intact.

Truby was taking the threat to blow Ben up right down to the wire.

He'd been out of that hut for two hours – time that could have been spent rescuing the hostages. All that time, wasted. Now that he was about to spend the night entombed in snow, Ben had nothing but feelings of sympathy for those buried by the avalanche.

What did it matter how rich they were, or how important? When it came down to it, they were just people; flesh and blood, and like everyone else, afraid to die.

Ben fell to his knees, utterly drained. If he'd had the energy for it or the tears, he might have wept from rage and frustration. As it was, he barely managed to crawl back into the snow cave, where he rolled clumsily onto the widest ledge. He curled up tightly and let heavy eyelids fall closed. Outside, he heard the cries of a flock of birds.

← CHOPPER ←

Ben's hands felt as though a thousand tiny needles were embedded in his skin. He couldn't even curl the rigid, crooked fingers into a fist. Every muscle ached from the effort of walking with a broken ankle across two hundred metres of snow that was never less than knee-deep. But not even total exhaustion brought sleep.

Between the unremitting shivers, as well as piercing discomfort from his broken ankle, he barely managed to lose consciousness for more than a few minutes at a time. Without his phone, he had to rely on his inner clock. If he'd been suited up for a rescue mission, Ben would have been wearing one of the Breitling timepieces that formed part of Gemini Force's kit. In his everyday life, however, like most people his age, he rarely wore a watch.

He woke up from a very brief doze and heard something different. At first he thought maybe it was the same birds he'd heard before. The more he tuned in, however, the more certain he became.

A helicopter.

Rushing to get out of the cave, Ben stumbled into the narrow trench outside. The shovel was still propped up against the wall he'd made in the snow pile. He grabbed it with trembling hands, steadied himself and looked into the sky.

It had to be Gemini Force. They'd received his distress signal. Ben leaned back against the wall of the snow cave. Relief washed over him. The silhouette of a helicopter passed in front of the full moon.

Finally.

There had to be at least four hours left on the clock. With their new ice-digging robot, Ben knew that Gemini Force would be able to reach the buried VIPs before they ran out of air.

It was over for #NEWGAME. The hostages would be rescued. Ben had *won*.

Dazed with feelings of victorious joy, it took him almost a minute to realise that his own life was still at stake.

He watched as the helicopter approached the spot farther down the slope, where his phone had almost certainly fallen. A blue-white beam of light pierced the darkness, trailing over the snow below him.

Ben climbed out of the trench. He began to yell, waving both arms. The chopper was slowly moving towards him, sweeping its searchlight. For a moment he wondered – why hadn't they detected his body heat with their infrared equipment? Had the cold of the snow cave masked any heat he'd given out while inside?

Seconds later the helicopter swooped over his position. Ben could only look on, helpless. Had they missed him? About fifty metres up the slope, the helicopter slowed to a pause. It hovered, almost touching the snow, lighting up a section directly below.

He held still, felt the buzz of the rotor blades as a vibration of the air on dry, chapped lips. Something was being dropped out of the helicopter. It was followed by a slight figure wearing skis. Then the aircraft was rotating in the air, until it was facing back down the slope.

He heard the unmistakeable sound of a dog barking. Rigel. The shadowy frame of a skier was making its way down the slope, dragging a sledge. Directly in front of the snow cave, the skier executed a dramatic parallel turn stop.

Jasmine's voice called out, 'Ben! You're all right!'

Seconds later he was almost knocked off his feet when Rigel bounced into him. Ben resisted wincing at the effort of remaining upright while Rigel nuzzled against his right leg. He heard Jasmine slip out of her ski bindings before she rushed over to him and threw both arms around his neck. He responded, hugging her back but not as eagerly as he'd have liked, because of having to keep weight off his right foot.

Jasmine didn't hold back. She clung to him, pressed kisses to his cheeks and neck, to every bit of exposed skin, all the while murmuring, 'Oh Ben, you're *freezing* . . .'

'You . . . you're *here*.' he mumbled, dazed.

'Of course, of course, JT sent Addi to fetch me as soon as we knew they'd taken you. Oh, *Ben*!' Jasmine hugged him tight, the heat of her skin searing his own cheek where they were pressed together.

He clutched the sides of Jasmine's ski suit and pushed her away just enough that he could speak. But he couldn't even get through the next sentence without his teeth chattering. 'Has . . . JT . . . begun . . . the rescue?'

She nodded, breathing rapidly. 'Yes, yes, the minute we got your signal. The Swiss police started shooting at the protestors.'

His voice sounded faint, even to himself. 'They . . . *killed* them?'

The sound of the helicopter's sudden approach muffled Jasmine's reply. In confusion, Ben turned his head, searching for the source of the pulsating rotor blade. Then he understood. It wasn't the helicopter that had brought Jasmine. That vehicle, he realised, was hovering around the lower reaches of the slope.

It was a second helicopter.

Ben's fingers tightened in Jasmine's ski suit. He stared at her, intently, concentrated on getting the words out smoothly despite his trembling jaw. 'D'you bring another chopper?'

He felt her gripping his shoulders even harder. 'Not that I know of.'

The second helicopter was headed straight for them, its searchlight dazzling in the midnight blue of the sky. Jasmine froze where she stood, her arms rigid against him.

A shudder went through him. Running was out of the question for him. Now Jasmine seemed to be paralysed with fear. Beside them, Rigel began to bark, leaping around. The sound of his warning appeared to unlock Jasmine's muscles. She wrenched herself away from him, scrambling back to her skis. Ben heard her boots clamp into the skis. He turned, faced down the approaching searchlight. Rigel yelped even louder. Ben took a shaky step towards Jasmine.

'Onto the sledge.' He could hear the tremor in her voice.

'Wait,' he muttered, moving sluggishly. 'My ankle's broken.'

Then it came. The sound ripped through crisp air, deafening as it echoed across the valley. Gunfire. Ben launched himself at Jasmine before she could utter a single cry. He knocked her to the ground, covering her body with his own. All around them, bullets zinged through the air and sizzled to a halt in deep snow. Beneath him, Ben felt Jasmine tremble. He raised his arms to protect her head, swept a lock of hair from her face with one finger. 'Shhh,' he whispered. 'No moving.'

For at least forty seconds, they remained motionless and silent, warming each other with their breath. Tentatively, Ben raised his head to see the hostile helicopter turn about a hundred metres away. It was preparing to return for a second run. From within the black depths of the nearby woods, he watched the first helicopter rise slowly into the air.

There was no doubt. The two pilots had spotted each other in the sky. It was between them, now.

This was the chance that Ben and Jasmine needed. He rocked forward onto his knees, held out a frozen hand to Jasmine, waited until she was upright before he rolled onto the sledge.

'The trees,' he managed to get out. 'As fast as you can.'

Pausing only to reach behind with both hands for the handle of the snow sledge, Jasmine pushed off and began to ski down the slope. As the sledge jumped forwards, Ben grabbed a handful of its loose Velcro ties. He twisted his wrists and fingers in the ties and held on tight.

The second helicopter was heading back up the slope towards their last position. A rattle of more bullets made them both shout out in alarm. Jasmine swerved for a moment, almost lost her balance. The sledge tilted to the left. Ben held his breath, leaned hard against the edge until he'd corrected its direction. Now they were hurtling down the mountain, two helicopters aiming straight for them, the closest one firing on the one that followed.

After her initial panic, Jasmine seemed to know exactly what to do. Her head was tucked in and she crouched low, weight forwards to maximise their velocity. Somewhere behind them, Ben heard Rigel bounding through the snow, letting loose an occasional strident bark.

Above them the air quivered as the nearest helicopter

shot overhead. It flew low enough that both Ben and Jasmine flinched. The shooting didn't stop. From what Ben could tell, it was one-way – the second arrival was raining bullets down on the helicopter that had brought Jasmine.

The sledge carved through the deep snow behind Jasmine's skis. In another few seconds they'd reach the cover of the trees. Ben's thoughts were already racing ahead, the pain of his right leg all but forgotten as adrenaline flooded his system. Gemini Force didn't carry weapons. Whoever was piloting the chopper was defenceless against the second helicopter's guns. And once the Gemini Force aircraft was out of the picture, Ben and Jasmine would be next.

The black shadows of hundreds of tall fir trees stretched across Ben's field of vision. Soon they were skiing into the heart of the thicket. Jasmine pulled up short, bent to unfasten her bindings as Ben rose to his feet. She turned to him frantically and grabbed his hands.

'Take cover!'

Moonlight streamed through the wood. It cast long, stark shadows into the ethereal glow that flowed between the towering fir trees.

Ben had his arms wrapped firmly around Jasmine, clinging onto her for the warmth of her body as much as for protection. She'd settled for pressing the side of her face to his. Her cheek felt like a hot water bottle against his face, which was still numb with cold.

They'd moved several trees deep into the woods and were crouched low behind the thickest trunk in the vicinity. The sounds of the two helicopters had receded into the distance, heading back towards the mountain. After a moment, Ben released Jasmine, took her right hand in his left. 'Come on. We need to be ready for a quick pick-up.'

Approaching the edge of the woods, both choppers came into clear view, framing the bright disc of the moon. They looked like black cockroaches rattling their wings as they drew closer to a light bulb.

At this distance, it was impossible to tell which was which. Ben could tell from Jasmine's anxious expression that she didn't know, either. One helicopter was drawing the other towards the summit of the mountain. An instant later, it had disappeared over the crest. The second helicopter followed, soaring upwards.

Then the silhouette of the first helicopter reappeared over the summit, just above where the hut must still be. Its searchlights burst into life. The second helicopter veered to the left in a last-minute attempt to escape collision. It tilted, hard. In the next moment, they were watching it tip over. They saw the flash of the explosion before they heard the booming rumble of the crash as the helicopter smashed into the wooden hut, shattering the building into a million splinters. A huge ball of flames bloomed like a chrysanthemum firework. For one brief moment, the entire left flank of the mountain lit up, bathed in tangerine light.

It was a few seconds before Ben could speak. 'Was that . . .?'

Jasmine was too stunned to respond. She clasped both hands to her mouth, eyes wide. The fireball was collapsing in on itself. A pall of black smoke rose in an almost straight line above the burning helicopter.

The remaining helicopter hadn't moved. It hovered like a bird of prey over the summit. Jasmine began to shrink further into the woods.

'Oh, no. If they've killed Addison . . .'

Ben leaned against the tree trunk. The pain of his broken ankle had escalated to a maddening level. He was gulping down gobbets of air just to stop himself from groaning aloud. He couldn't run. He wasn't even sure if he could drag himself back to where they'd left the sledge.

'If they've killed Addison then I've had it,' he said, wearily, pressing his forehead into the damp bark. 'But you need to go, Jasmine. Right now. Leave the sledge. I'll only slow you down.'

Jasmine gasped. She clutched at his arm. 'No . . . no,' she said, stammering. 'Together. We stay together.'

He reached for Jasmine, tangled her fingers clumsily with his own. 'You've already risked your life to save me. You need to go *now*, and you need to go fast. Rigel can stay here with me. He'll protect me, keep me warm until you can get help.'

Ben stopped talking then because the helicopter was on the move again. It was flying down from the summit, on a steady, direct approach. Any minute now it would find a place to land outside the woods, where the slope of the mountain became almost horizontal.

When he turned to Jasmine, he saw that she'd already gone. He pulled away from the tree trunk, peered through the woods until he spotted her. She'd snapped her boots back into the skis and was removing collapsible ski poles from her small backpack. She stood for a moment, just staring at him.

He waved her off. 'Go!'

A shadow in the moonlight; with a soft swish of her skis she was gone.

The helicopter's searchlight had begun to penetrate the woods. Ben held himself rigid, sheltering behind another tree. Rigel fell quiet, nuzzling him, rubbing himself back and forth against Ben's legs, which stung from the deep cold. Their breath rose in a pale white vapour. A torch would easily pick out such a giveaway sign of life. Assuming that whoever was about to search for him didn't have infrared equipment, which was a strong possibility.

As the helicopter landed, the outer branches of the nearby trees fluttered in the wind. Ben heard the heavy thrum of the rotor blades slowing. He held his breath.

Here it comes.

Then, through a megaphone, came Addison's voice. 'Ben? Jasmine? You guys OK?'

He sank down onto his haunches. All the tension left his body. After a few seconds his voice, choked up at first, eventually returned. He began to scream Jasmine's name.

She's OK. Addi is OK!

Addison looked pale and drawn as she helped Ben into the helicopter. He was careful not to praise what must have been a pretty impressive bit of flying, turning the helicopter so fast that it could just appear like that. Not to mention, *crazy-brave*. Like some demented game of chicken, and better never mentioned again, he suspected. The occupants of that second helicopter had fried to death, tricked into a deadly mistake by her daredevil manoeuvre. Ben knew perfectly well that Addi had left the US Air Force precisely to avoid being involved in any killing.

'You had no choice,' he told her, watching the taut set of her jaw as she piloted the helicopter into the air once again. 'They were armed. You weren't.'

She was quiet for a long time before she replied. 'I guess. Or maybe once a killer, always a killer,' she said, her voice low and regretful.

'You'd be dead,' Ben reminded her, softly. 'And Minos Winter would be coming for me and Jasmine.'

'It was Minos Winter?' Addison seemed to have no idea that they'd been dealing with the mercenary. *Of course not*, Ben thought. The video they'd sent had used a disguised voice.

'He was the one who abducted me. Although I'm pretty sure that Holden White set me up,' Ben added. He looked into the rear passenger section of the helicopter, where Jasmine sat cuddling Rigel.

'So – Minos Winter is dead,' Addison murmured. It didn't sound as though she was sorry. But then again, the man had once threatened to kill her, Julia and Ben.

'Makes you wonder what kind of society those #NEWGAME nutjobs are planning,' Ben commented. 'If they're happy to use a guy like Winter to get things done.'

Addison seemed to consider her reply. 'I think that when you've decided to cold-bloodedly murder innocent people to make an ideological point, you can be counted on to put all available weapons on the table. That's what Minos Winter is to them – just another weapon.'

'"The ends justify the means",' Ben muttered, bitterly.

The pilot nodded, soberly. 'Something like that.'

From the back of the helicopter, Jasmine was gazing at him in silence, one arm still draped around Rigel. She stretched out a hand to him. After a moment, Ben reached out and interlaced his fingers with hers.

They remained like that for a long time.

'Have to admit it – I did not think I'd end up watching this rescue on TV.'

Ben relaxed as a nurse removed the intravenous drip that ran into his hand. Beside him Jasmine tried to smile. 'Even if your ankle wasn't broken and you weren't half-boy, half-popsicle, I doubt if, uh, *Gemini,*' she said, careful to use Truby's secret call sign. 'You know, I doubt that he'd let you anywhere near the rescue. Your face has been all over the news ever since #NEWGAME broadcast that video of you being put in the mountain hut.'

'But I saw that video,' he objected '– it didn't show my face'.

'The one they sent to the TV networks had all this extra stuff about you. All about your mother, footage from that rescue the two of you did on the Sky High Hotel. Photos from your school lacrosse team. Photos of you from the cocktail party at the World Economic Forum.'

'That's how Minos Winter found out who I am,' Ben said, nodding. 'It was all there, I guess. Just waiting for him to make the connection between who he saw on the *PSV Macondo* – and Gemini Force.'

'The video they broadcast ended with that clip of you alone on the mountain, looking up at the helicopter that dropped you there.' Jasmine risked another smile. 'If it hadn't been *you*, I'd have found it incredibly exciting.'

'Yeah well trust me, less exciting, more *terrifying*,' Ben said, ruefully.

She held his gaze for a moment, her eyes gentle and filled with affection. 'Also - you're all over the Internet. Seriously. There are tumblrs about you. My favourite is called *heckyeahbencarrington*. They have animated GIF sets and everything. You look very handsome. I guess you're going to have a lot of girls writing to you now. Boys, too, probably.'

Ben had no idea how to respond to this. The idea of that type of fame was kind of horrifying but also a little bit cool. 'Um – yay?' he said, testing Jasmine's reaction. To his relief, she broke into a huge grin. 'It actually made things easier with Jonah, after we broke up. He sent me a text, you wanna read it?'

Then she was showing him her phone.

Just saw Benedict Carrington on TV. OK I admit it he's pretty cool. If I have to lose out to someone it might as well be him.

'That's rather gracious of him,' Ben admitted. 'Not sure I'd take it so well.'

Jasmine pursed her lips, suppressing a smile. 'Oh really? What would you do?'

Ben took her hand and tugged gently, drawing her into his arms. 'I'd fight him for you.'

'Wouldn't be a very fair fight,' she murmured, blinking slowly enough that he found himself melted by the warmth of her eyes. 'With all that *krav maga* you've been practising.'

'S'perfectly fair,' he muttered, against her cheek.

Their attention returned to the television screen that was mounted on a pull-out arm attached to the wall opposite.

GF Nine was being shown in close-up now, positioned over the person-sized hole it had dug from the surface of the snow pile that the avalanche had dumped onto the coaches. The footage was clearly being shot with a long lens, since every so often a uniformed member of Gemini Force could be seen guarding the vehicle from within the rescue site, which had been cordoned off by police tape. Just the same, Ben was alarmed at the level of detail that was being shown. Combined with the live recording of the entire digging operation, there'd be enough material here for other people to build something similar to Gemini Force's 'Iceman'.

'*Gemini* must be furious,' he said, snapping his mouth shut when a nurse entered the room.

Jasmine waited for the nurse to clear away the dressings. They both gave the young Swiss woman a smile as she left. Then she said, 'He is. My dad says that JT is fuming like a volcano. But it could be worse. As things are, you're the only one that anyone will recognise. The terrorists didn't name JT or anyone else in the agency.'

'But they *know*,' Ben said, puzzled. 'They know about JT and they've guessed about Addi.'

Jasmine raised an eyebrow. 'Really? How come?'

'JT – I guess it's his connection with my mother. Plus, there can't be many people with the money to create something like Gemini Force. Addi, well, she was at the Sky High,' he said, sounding doleful. 'And she was in the Caroliners. It wasn't too hard to work it out. Minos Winter got a good look at me, Julia and Addison.'

'Maybe they have a reason to keep any other names out of the reports?'

He groaned. 'Yeah, it probably involves extorting money out of someone.'

She covered his hand with her own and looked into Ben's eyes. 'Don't sound so glum. None of this is your fault.'

Ben glanced away, unwilling to let her see the weight of disappointment in his expression. 'It's not that. It's just . . . Isn't it obvious? I'm going to be a liability now. JT's not going to be able to allow me on any missions.'

'Why not?'

'Because, hello? *Secrecy*.'

'That's ridiculous. If you put a helmet and goggles on, no one would be able to tell it's you.'

He squeezed her hand, gently, and gestured towards

the TV screen. 'Even with that kit on I can tell that it's James, Paul and Toru.'

'That's only because you know them,' she pointed out.

Jasmine was right, but Ben couldn't help but feel, with a sinking heart, that in one crucial way, the glory days of Gemini Force were over. Now, their every movement would be followed by the world's media. Discovering the secret identities of each member of the team would become an internationally popular guessing game. Their rescues would be filmed by mobile phones and appear on the Internet within minutes. Envious business rivals would hassle suppliers to give away the secrets of their technology. Who could say – maybe even their secret location might be compromised?

They could only hope that Truby's high level contacts in the world's governments might provide some protection.

He sighed. The TV screen was now showing the hostages emerging one by one, raised on safety harnesses. Most were conscious, although their faces looked pale and drawn. At least one person, a man in his seventies, was stretchered away immediately, totally immobile.

A female news reporter was saying, 'Concern for his health mounts as Gennady Krupin, president of the Russian investment bank *Mozno*, is taken away on a stretcher. It's thought that the sixty-four-year-old financier, often referred to as "the oligarch's oligarch", suffered a heart attack in the past hour, during which oxygen levels are said to have fallen dangerously low inside both of the buried coaches here in Davos.'

'At least they saved the *oligarchs*,' Ben muttered sarcastically, leaning back on the stack of pillows.

'You think they should have left them there?'

'Course not. Why d'you think I risked my life getting out of the mountain hut as fast as I possibly could? It was the only way to get Gemini Force to stop hanging about, waiting to see what Minos Winter was prepared to let us do. I knew that if I could let JT know that I'd escaped, he would start the rescue.'

'He wouldn't have sacrificed you,' Jasmine began, shaking her head.

Ben shrugged. 'All I knew for sure was that if JT knew I'd made it out of there, Gemini Force would get to work. Winter's sick game of chicken would be over.'

He was acting more blasé than he really felt, though. Ben knew, deep down, that he'd wondered whether Truby would be prepared to sacrifice him. Inside the hut, he'd sensed the hair-trigger of explosive death just around the corner.

An elderly woman was being wheeled along the corridor by the same, sweet-faced nurse who'd moments ago visited his room. Ben looked at them for a moment. He didn't want to watch the rescue on TV any longer. All it did was remind him that one way or another, everything was going to be different from now on.

Ben wasn't even sure that he'd be allowed to stay in Gemini Force.

─ GAME CHANGER ─

Outside the Hotel le Dauphin and once again, Holden White was holding court.

'Doubt my music,' the singer announced to the assembled crowd. 'Doubt my talent, if you want. I couldn't give a monkey's, to be honest. I do it for me; I do it for the fans. But do *not* doubt my sincerity. I meant every word I said about what's wrong with the world.'

Wearing black jeans and a long, black mohair sweater over a black shirt, only White's hair and beard betrayed signs of stress, with dark roots showing beneath the bleach. Ben hadn't seen the singer look quite so rumpled since the last time he saw him live on stage.

Reporters had been waiting outside the hotel, held at bay by the security guards. Now they'd ambushed White and the four Swiss police who'd come to arrest him. To his credit, White seemed to be handling the whole thing fairly well, using the chance to put his case.

Almost as if he'd anticipated it.

Jasmine and Ben had just been dropped off after he'd been discharged from hospital. From the taxi rank, Ben watched discreetly, leaning on his crutches. He doubted that White had noticed them.

White spoke again, gesticulating with his left hand.

'These VIPs being rescued by Gemini Force or whatever – it doesn't change a thing. It's coming, mark my words. Real change. People like Gennady Krupin won't sleep safe in their beds from now on. And nor should they.'

A huddle of press and paparazzi exploded with questions then, voices yelling across each other to be heard. As the tumult finally calmed down, a Swiss police captain took over. 'That's enough. Mr White has agreed to answer some questions down at the station. Please be so kind as to make space for us to leave.'

Then White was snatching back the spotlight. A strange, imploring note entered his voice. 'I didn't know, mate. *Ben*. I mean it. They said they just wanted to *talk*.'

Ben could see White staring directly at him. There was a pleading look in the man's eyes. The Swiss police began forging a path through the reporters. But one of them must have turned to follow White's gaze, because suddenly the shout went up, 'Benedict Carrington! Ben Carrington is here!'

Before he'd properly registered that most of the reporters and photographers were in the process of dashing across the short stretch of pavement between them and the revolving doors to the hotel, Ben felt Jasmine grab his hand. She yanked him towards the revolving doors and pushed him through. A second later his left crutch had jammed the mechanism and he was jiggling it back and forth against the angled glass door, trying to free himself. Jasmine followed him inside where they ended up staring through the glass doors, appalled.

Outside the hotel, it was a free-for-all as paparazzi practically crawled over each other to take a decent snap of the teenagers. Some were even reckless enough to try to push past the stocky security guards.

'That was weird,' Ben breathed, as they headed for the hotel lifts. 'I guess it's because I told the police that White was there when Minos Winter snatched me.'

He'd fallen short of telling them that he suspected White's role in the incident. Somehow, Ben just couldn't bring himself to grass on his favourite singer. But it seemed that the police had come to that conclusion anyway.

Was White telling the truth? If he was, then Truby would be right, Ben realised with a surge of regret – the singer would have to be a colossal fool.

At least it was better than being a terrorist.

Whatever Jasmine had been thinking about, Ben's comment seemed to distract her. 'You really think Holden White set you up?'

'I didn't say that . . . but going on what Holden just said to me, I'm guessing that the police might think he did. And I guess he's saying that he didn't.'

'Do you believe him?'

Ben exhaled slowly, unable to respond.

'I'm sorry,' Jasmine said, after a moment of silence. 'I'm sorry that your hero disappointed you.'

He snorted, 'Holden White wasn't my hero.'

The lift doors opened. As they stepped inside, Jasmine blocked the button panel with one arm. 'Look, I've been thinking about this. You can't go back to your room. One of those reporters probably has an informer inside the hotel. You can't be seen with Truby now.'

The implications of Jasmine's words sunk in and Ben said, 'Because they don't know that JT is part of Gemini Force?'

'You're the only one they're sure about.'

As far as Gemini Force was concerned, even one publicly recognisable member of the team was a game-changer. 'We need to get out of here.'

Jasmine pressed the button for the basement. 'There has to be a way out via the underground car park. The minute you get phone signal again, you should call JT, tell him we're getting a taxi to the airfield and to bring your stuff.'

Five minutes later they were sneaking out of the fire exit which led from the underground car park. While Ben tried to be as inconspicuous as possible, pressed up against the freezing concrete wall, Jasmine sneaked out towards the front of the hotel. She returned in a taxi, half a dozen photographers chasing the car. Ben flung both crutches through the open rear passenger door before hurling himself bodily after them. Jasmine leaned across him and grabbed the door handle. She was just in time to let the taxi driver rocket them away before one of the paparazzi could stop them.

As Jasmine slid back over him, Ben caught her in his arms. He managed to land a quick kiss, which just missed her mouth as she turned her face away, smiling.

'*Thank* you,' he said. He'd definitely caught her by surprise, which pleased him. But Jasmine recovered after a few seconds and wrapped both arms around his neck. 'What for?'

Ben shrugged. 'Oh, y'know, everyday saviour stuff. Rescuing me on the mountain. Coming to visit me in hospital.'

'Hmm,' she said. He could feel her eyes examining him. 'You'd do the same for me.'

'I most certainly would.' He hesitated, suddenly wary. This was a good time to mention it and he was feeling exceptionally brave. 'And of course, the little matter of "I love you".'

'Oh,' she said, gasping slightly. 'That.'

Ben forced himself not to flinch from her gaze. 'Do you?' he added, haltingly. 'Or was it a heat-of-the-moment thing?'

A delicate blush spread over her features. Ben felt himself respond in kind. He cracked first, allowing an embarrassed chuckle to escape him. 'Yeah, I guessed it was too good to be true.'

'It's not that. I mean – maybe. But . . . urrgh! Timing! I don't like that I said it over the phone. Can we pretend I didn't say it?'

He froze. This wasn't what he'd expected. 'Sure . . .' he tried to say, but almost choked.

'Hey. I mean – it should be romantic, yes? Like, we should be on top of a mountain or something.'

His expression cleared. 'Ah! Yes. Somewhere dramatic.'

'Not in the back of a taxi, either.'

Ben grinned, relaxing. 'Fair enough. There's a rather nice restaurant on top of the Weissfluh. Hint, hint.' He really wanted to lock down the whole girlfriend situation.

It was too nerve racking, not knowing whether Jasmine was his girl or not.

'Oh, I know,' she replied, airily. 'And FYI, I like pink roses and milk chocolate.'

'Me too,' he agreed. 'You can put a tick in that box.'

'So,' she added, casually, using one hand to ruffle his hair, 'you think I should join Gemini Force?'

Ben pulled her closer. 'We're still looking for an *Aries*.'

A playful grin was on her lips. 'But what if I decide I want to be an international banker?'

'That *would* be rather Swiss of you,' he agreed and leaned in for his second attempt at a kiss. 'But "chocolate-maker" would be so much better.'

⤙ POSTER BOY ⤚

'We're landing already?'

Ben shifted in his seat, trying to get a visual fix on one of the navigation screens in the cockpit area of GF Two. Jasmine had chosen one of the seats that faced the equipment bay, and he'd taken the seat next to hers. He'd been enjoying a close-up view of GF Nine – 'Iceman'. Gemini Force's newest addition was now fully-powered with the device that Truby had bought from the CERN research institute they'd visited just a week ago. The machine had successfully smashed through ice and snow and tunnelled directly to the buried coaches using a combination of infrared and microwave radiation to locate and reveal the vehicle.

He'd assumed that they were returning to GF One. Yet, *Leo* wasn't heading for the sub-orbital flight path that would take them across the Atlantic Ocean in less than three hours. If anything, they were losing altitude.

'C'mon,' he said, 'I can tell you know something. Where are we going?'

'I can't say,' Jasmine said, giggling as Ben dug two fingers into her ribs, threatening to tickle her into giving him an answer. 'Don't make me! I *promised*.'

Ben withdrew his hand, still holding her gaze. 'All

right,' he said, darkly. 'But it had better be something to do with chocolate. That's the only thing worth staying in this country for, now that I can't ski.'

Sitting opposite them both, Addison looked up from her e-reader. 'Oh, we've already left Switzerland.'

'I get it: you're all in on this?'

'Yesirree Bob,' replied Addi, with a smirk. 'And what's more, we brought special outfits.'

'Outfits?' Ben was even more mystified than before. The aircraft was landing now, in vertical mode. Impatiently pushing against his seat belt while Toru completed the landing, Ben strained to see anything through the windows. There was nothing except the pitch black of night.

Once the full interior lights went on, Ben unfastened his seat belt, picked up the two crutches that he'd leaned against his seat and stood up. With mounting curiosity he watched as Addison, James and Paul busied themselves with retrieving black plastic suit-carriers from the equipment lockers.

'What kind of outfits?' he said, falling into step beside Addison. No one replied. Jason Truby was following a few paces behind, next to Jasmine, who'd stalled to release Rigel from his cage. The dog ambled off, happily joining up with the leading group at GF Two's exit.

'Ready, Ben?' Truby said, with a grin.

'Ready for what?' Ben blurted, leaning forward against his crutches. He wasn't bothering to hide his eagerness and frustration – not from this motley crew, who seemed bent on watching whatever surprise awaited their youngest colleague.

And the smirks continued.

Then *Leo's* door was opening onto the moonlit outdoors. The air was crisp, dry; very cold, and the black outlines of distant, craggy mountain peaks stretched before them. Ben began to make out the shapes of stone buildings bathed in moonlight.

'Wait, what are we doing here?' he began, mystified. 'This looks like . . .'

'Wait, wait,' Truby said. Ben turned to see Truby waving something that looked like a remote control in the direction of the buildings. Arc lights buried in the ground came suddenly alive, flooding the stone buildings of Ben's ancestral home with golden light.

Ben gasped. 'Schloss Bach,' he said, softly.

'The realtor gave me a great price,' Truby said, not quite looking at Ben as he spoke. 'Yeah, the current Count Brandis sold it to my realtor . . . I'm pretty happy with the deal. I hope he was too.'

In quiet amazement, Ben turned to him. 'You bought my grandpa's Schloss.'

'Well, I needed a European base,' Truby explained. 'Your mom had the right idea, I think. Mountain rescue needs to be its own thing.'

Ben picked up his crutches and flipped the ice spikes into position on each. He stepped cautiously out onto the steps that led to the snow-covered ground, following first Rigel, then Addison, James, Paul and Toru. Bathed in tawny lighting against the silvery star-scape of the night sky, Schloss Bach looked spectacular. He couldn't help but imagine what his mother would have made of the sight of their ancestral home looking like a miniature Palace of Versailles.

'You've made it look amazing,' he admitted to Truby, and added sincerely, 'thank you. Mum would have liked this. She'd have loved it.'

'We made some changes inside too,' Truby said, lightly. Ben was still hanging back, drinking in the view. Gratitude swelled within him as he realised the extent of Truby's actions.

Jasmine took his elbow. 'Come on, Ben,' she said, softly. 'Let's go in.'

Truby escorted them through the grand entrance to the house, now decorated with the two stone lions that Ben's grandfather had found broken and half-buried in the garden after the vandalism of the departing Nazis. The figures had been restored and stood proudly as sentinels in front of the main door. A flag hung on either side – Austrian on one side, USA on the other.

'Nice,' he said, quietly, acknowledging the symbolism of the gesture. Austria and the USA. As if to suggest that this might have become *their* home – Truby's and Caroline's – if she'd lived. 'She'd have liked that, too.'

A brand new rug adorned the polished oak floor of the entrance hall, whose walls had been freshly painted in salmon and white. On two occasional tables, stoneware vases held bunches of red and white geraniums, which gave off a spicy aroma. Ben and Jasmine followed Truby into the dining room, its cream-coloured walls delicately edged with a fresh coat of gilt decoration. From the ceiling hung three wrought iron and glass chandeliers, restored so that each glass jewel shone with brilliant light from the candles that adorned each tier.

Around the room, Ben recognised various paintings which had been sold along with the house. The twenty-seater table, solid mahogany with a French polish, had been set for seven, complete with a white damask table cloth, napkins, antique silver cutlery, and crystal hurricane vases with alternating red and white roses. Six silver candlesticks were set with burning beeswax candles that filled the air with the sweet scent of honey.

Jasmine clasped a hand to his. 'Oh, Ben! It's so beautiful!'

Ben remained speechless. The way the house had been decorated, the table setting, the whole dining room – it was all worthy of his mother, Countess Caroline. He glanced at Truby, who was watching him closely. 'This is amazing, Jason. I don't know how to thank you. I . . . I could never have made it like this. But this is exactly how Mum would have wanted it.'

'Hey, you've got different priorities, kid. I like your priorities, too. You'll go out and supervise those schools you're building in Africa, before too long.' Truby placed a steady palm on Ben's shoulder. 'Since you're here, maybe Count Brandis can entertain some guests in his ancestral home?'

'Ha,' Ben snorted. It still sounded strange to be referred to that way. 'Actually, where did they all go?'

'They went to get changed into tuxedos,' Truby said. 'For you, I got something special.'

As he spoke, a teenage member of the domestic staff emerged from the kitchen. He wore a dark suit with a stiff white shirt. In one hand he held a hanger draped with a pair of black trousers, a white dress shirt and a traditional Styrian jacket. In silence, the boy regarded Ben with cold blue eyes that barely flickered in recognition.

It was the Austrian boy from the gym, the one who'd offered Ben an impromptu boxing match.

'I made sure that it's the right type of jacket for this region,' continued Truby. He was oblivious to the fact that the boys had recognised each other. 'After all, you *are* the Count.'

Ben rested on both crutches, examining the suit. His lips twitched slightly, suppressing a grin. 'It's perfect,' he said, quietly, with a nod at Truby. He glanced up again, looked directly at the serving boy. 'Hullo again.' He made to turn away and then paused. In German, he asked the teenager. 'About that offer to spar . . . Would you, uh . . . would you maybe like to learn some *krav maga,* sometime?'

The boy's cheeks flushed. With difficulty, he nodded, stiffly. 'Yeah. That'd be OK.' He nodded, curtly. 'I'll take your suit to your room,' he said, with a glance at Ben's crutches. With a quick bow, the boy headed for the staircase.

Jasmine yawned. 'I'm going to change for dinner.'

Before Truby could follow her upstairs, Ben said, 'Jason, I need to know. Would you have let Gemini Force make the rescue? If I hadn't escaped, I mean. Would you still have rescued those people?'

Truby seemed surprised at the question. His olive-green eyes narrowed for a moment, studying Ben's face. 'You're asking me if I'd have let those cowards blow apart the hut with you inside?'

'I wouldn't blame you,' Ben said. There was more resignation in his voice than he'd intended.

'The truth is, Ben, *I don't know*. I stopped the Swiss cops from shooting the protestors; I told them that Gemini Force wouldn't rescue those folk if they spilled any blood.'

'You'd have let them die, all those important people . . . I know you knew some of them, Jason. You'd really have let them suffocate, to save me?'

'Listen to me, Ben. What I knew for sure is this: that you'd get out of there,' Truby said, with conviction. 'I knew I could count on you. The Benedict Carrington that I know – the son of Caroline Carrington – he does *not* sit on his ass, waiting to die.'

'Well, that's true.' Ben managed a wan smile. 'So, Jason – me and Gemini Force. I realise things might be tricky at this point.'

'Tricky? Yeah, a little bit. You're famous, Ben. I guess the helmets are going to be mandatory for rescues, now.'

'We're still cool, then?'

'We're very cool,' Jason replied, evenly. '*Taurus* – he's gonna be the public face of Gemini Force. The poster boy.'

'Hmm,' Ben said. 'Not sure I fancy that.'

He thought about the traditional Austrian suit that was waiting for him upstairs, thought about his great-grandparents who'd lost their home because they'd defied the Nazis, of his grandfather returning to try to resurrect the family home, of his mother, Caroline, who'd dedicated herself to the same project; of family traditions and buildings and how they were continued by each generation, how for him those traditions would be continued not in the cold mountains of central Europe, but among the arid plains of Africa, with and for young friends he'd made inside one of the deepest mines on the planet. And finally, his thoughts turned to the grand project of Jason Truby – Gemini Force. There too, Ben now understood, he could have an impact.

Bending to stroke Rigel's head, after a minute, Ben straightened up. 'Poster boy, really?'

Truby's amusement reached the edges of his mouth but no further. 'Would you prefer "spokesman"? Especially now that we have a European base?'

Ben allowed himself a genuine smile. 'If that's what Gemini Force needs from me,' he said, 'then sure. Why not?'